THE DESTINED

Book Three

THE KEEPER TRILOGY

KAY CHANDLER
A multi-Award-winning author

This is a work of fiction. Characters, places and incidents are the products of the author's imagination or are used fictitiously. Scripture from Holy Bible, KJV

Cover Design by Chase Chandler

DEDICATED TO THE FOLLOWING BIKERS

Clyde Varmint Hornsby, Joe Childs, Teresa Register Roach, Larry Harrison, Sue Early, Norman Childs, Edmon Devon Blocker, Sandra Reagan, Annie Ruth Judy, Warren Tomberlin, Bobbie Ashworth, Jack Dykema, Kim Harrison, Redetha Reagan Stewart, Barbara B. Bryan, Martha Childs, Linda Aycock, Sue McGee Work, Huberta Merritt, Shelley Guinn, Deborah Crocker, Gayle Courtney, Mitch and Brandy Herrington

Your input was much appreciated. Your friendship, even more. Thank you!

CHAPTER 1

Everything Cami Gorham believed in was a lie. The man she believed to be her father was not her father. The mother she believed to be a saint was a sinner. And the wealthy lifestyle she'd taken for granted, she recently learned was financed with stolen funds. How could she have been so deceived?

With her designer backpack thrown over her shoulder, she tossed her phone, then sprinted to the nearest Interstate exit with no clue where she was going, how she'd get there, or what she'd do when she arrived. Standing near the edge of the pavement, Cami threw up her thumb, recalling the way Claudette Colbert did it in *It Happened One Night*—an old black and white movie classic she'd watched more than once.

A dozen or more vehicles zoomed past but she wouldn't give

up. Couldn't give up. After all, Claudette didn't have luck right away, either. It took patience. Had her attention not been focused on the tractor-trailer coming over the hill in the distance, perhaps she would've seen the motorcycle veering off the highway in her direction. It swerved, then slammed to a stop between her and the pavement, stirring up a thick cloud of dust. Feigning a disgusted shiver, she glared at the biker, then wiped the taste of dust from her lips with the back of her hand.

He lifted his helmet. Dark, tousled curls hung between twinkling blue eyes. "Ah, I see you waited for me."

She knew arrogance when she saw it, and this dude was full of it. Perhaps he was accustomed to girls being flattered when he graced them with his presence, but he'd not only picked the wrong time but the wrong girl. With his striking good looks it was understandable why he'd have such an enormous ego. Maybe another time, another place, she could've been interested. But not now. Not here.

Pearly white teeth sparkled against his tanned face when he smiled. "I'm glad I'm not too late."

"Not as late as I would've preferred," she smirked. Cami thrust out her thumb and attempted to ignore him in the hopes he'd leave as quickly as he'd approached.

"You thumbing?"

It wasn't so much the stupid question as the infuriating way he chuckled afterward. Such ignorance didn't require a response. With her chin tilted upward, she stepped in front of the bike, and thrust her arm out as far as she could reach. The oncoming truck slowed, but when the biker waved him off, the driver threw up his hand and left her standing there.

She plunked her hands on her hips and scowled. "Now, see what you've done? That truck would've stopped if you hadn't been here."

"You know, I think you're right. Lucky for you I came along when I did."

"Are you nuts? I want you to leave."

"Can't."

"What do you mean, you *can't?*"

"Woman, do you have any idea the dangerous game you're playing?"

"I figured it out the minute you stopped. Unless you're my Guardian Angel, I'd be grateful if you'd leave."

He hopped off his bike, reached in his shirt pocket and pulled out a piece of gum. He slowly unwrapped it, then popped it in his mouth. He held out the pack. "You chew?"

"No!" She licked her dry lips. Her jaw jutted forward when he plopped down on the ground next to her and leaned against a fence post, as if he'd arrived at his destination. "What do you think you're doing?"

"Making sure you don't do something stupid. Just call me Gabriel."

"I suppose you think you're funny but you're not. Please, go. It's getting late, and I need to get away before—"

"Before what?"

"Before I'm forced to go back where I don't belong. Look, mister, I'm sorry for being rude. You caught me in a lousy mood. I'm sure you're a good guy and think you're doing me a favor, but I've got to get out of town before they discover I'm gone." She took a few steps backward after a commercial bus came close to mowing off her toes.

"Running from the cops?"

"Seriously? Do I look like a criminal to you? Not that I owe you an explanation but it's a complicated family issue."

"Then what are we waiting for? Hop on the back of my bike and we'll be outta here in two shakes."

She eyed the big, shiny blue bike and lifted her lip in a snarl. "You can't be serious. Ride on the back of that monster with bugs flying in my face? Thanks, but no way. Now, please go. No one will stop if they see a guy with me. They'll assume . . ."

His face split into a craggy smile. "Assume I stopped to help? They'll be right. I understand you feel desperate, but try using a little common sense. You're a fairly nice-looking woman and it's a given that *someone* will stop to pick you up. A human trafficker, a crazed druggie, a sex predator, a serial killer . . . or just maybe a guy on a bike whose only motive is to keep your name out of tomorrow's obits."

She stiffened. What did he mean by fairly nice-looking? Plenty of guys considered her beautiful. Was his choice of words just another way to antagonize her?

He stood, brushed himself off, and walked over to his bike.

Grateful that he decided to leave, yet a deep sense of guilt gnawed at her insides. As much as she fought the urge, she couldn't deny an apology was in order. "Hey, I'm sorry for being snarky. I know you meant well and your concern is noted, though unwarranted."

"Gotcha. And I accept your apology, ma'am."

"Then we're good?"

"Yep."

"I'm glad." She gave a slight wave of her hand. "Have a safe trip."

"Thank you, ma'am. I'd begun to think you didn't care." He took a paper sack from a saddlebag, pulled out two wrapped sandwiches, then walked back over to the tree. "I didn't eat lunch and I'm starved."

She ran her hands through her hair. "You had no thoughts of leaving, did you?"

"Nope, but I have as much time as you do, so we'll go whenever you're ready." He held out a sandwich in each hand. "Peanut Butter or cheese?"

She stomped her foot. "You are so exasperating."

"I'd say you're very perceptive. Hey, I have an idea. Why don't we do half and half? Half PB&J and half cheese? Sound good?"

The pungent smell of Peanut Butter filled her nostrils. Cami couldn't deny it did sound good. She reached out and grabbed half a sandwich.

His upper lip curled in a smile. "Atta girl. Now, hurry and eat. We need to get to the shop and suit you up before it closes. You can't ride in that silly get-up you're wearing."

"You really expect me to get on that monster, don't you?" What choice did she have? Except for the one truck, no one had even slowed. She eyed the huge piece of metal held up by two wheels and weighed the consequences. Not dismissing the strong possibility she wouldn't live to see the next sunrise if she crawled on the back of the bike, but going back home would be a fate she considered worse than death. "Fine. But there's no need to suit me up, as you call it. I happen to like what I'm wearing."

"I'm sure you do, but trust me, you wouldn't by the time we get to where we're going."

"I must be crazy," she murmured, settling on the back seat. "Don't go fast. Please? I'm scared."

"Nothing to be afraid of." He raced the motor. "Trust me, you'll love it."

She muttered a quick prayer, then reached into a side pocket on her backpack and pulled out a scarf to tie around her hair and face. The bike leaped as they sped away. She squealed, grabbed him around the waist and held tightly.

Parking on the side of a strip mall, he jumped off and extended his hand. "Give me your backpack, and hurry before Dak locks up."

"Why?"

"I'll strap it to my bag. You won't need it inside."

"What if someone steals it?"

"No one comes here but bikers. We don't steal from one another."

"So, you're a bunch of Robin Hoods of the Harley Forrest? Only steal from others?" She slid her arms from the straps. "If this is gone when we get back, you'll . . ."

"Would you stop whimpering and come on? Dak closes in about thirty minutes."

He helped her off the bike, then walked her to the door and held it open. "You really are Gabriel, aren't you?"

"Yes ma'am, your guardian angel at your service. But I like to remain incognito, so I use the alias, Ian, when on earthly duty."

She giggled. "It'll be our secret. I'm Camille, Ian. My friends call me Cami."

They stepped inside and the shop owner rushed toward Ian with an outstretched hand. "Ian Benrey! Had you on my mind all day. Wondered if you'd be stopping by on your way back to the mountains. Good to see you man. And who is your pretty traveling companion?"

"Dak, I'd like you to meet . . . "

She swallowed hard. What if the man recognized her from pictures on the Social Page in *The Virginia Reel News?*

Ian's gaze met hers. "Dak, meet Kimi. We need you to outfit her for our trip. Vent jacket, pants, boots, helmet . . . the works."

11

Cami pressed her lips together. *Did he say Kimi?* Maybe Ian really was her guardian angel.

Dak was short and a little on the heavy side, with a smile that made her feel as if shed known him all her life. He held out his hand. "Nice to meet you, ma'am. So, Kimi, I'm guessing you're a local, since you'd be suited up if you weren't just beginning the journey. What's your last name? I've lived here for years and know most folks in the area."

She stammered.

Ian winked. "Just call us the Benreys, Dak. Sounds cool, doesn't it?"

The shop owner grinned and slapped Ian across the back. "Well blow me down, you ol' son of a gun. You done gone and jumped the broom. You sure got you a prize, I'll have to say that." He tossed several odd pieces of clothing into a cart, which Cami considered quite useless. "Here ya' go, Mrs. Benrey. The dressing room is in the back. Ian, you can go back and help your bride, if you like."

"Well, that's mighty kind of you, brother, but she's a little shy, so I'll wait for her out here. That okay with you, darlin'?"

"Perfectly okay, *sweetheart.*"

After putting on the last garb, Cami twirled around in front of the mirror several times and let the wonderful smell of leather fill her nostrils. She might hate the bike ride, but she couldn't deny she loved the apparel . . .the jeans, the feel of the leather, the silver zippers on the vent jacket, and the boots were all so cool. Dak even threw in a durag, which made her giggle. Next, he'd be suggesting she traipse down to the tattoo parlor.

CHAPTER 2

Taking one last glance in the mirror, Cami stepped out of the dressing room. The look of approval on Ian's face warmed her heart, though she quickly conceded it would be naïve to think she was the only woman he looked at with the same gleam in his eye. No doubt his warm smile had melted more than a few hearts.

His lip curled upward at the corner. "Wow, you look awesome . . . dear."

Cami tried to hide her smile, but she'd never had a man look at her with such tenderness. What was it with this guy? Why was he being so good to her? She didn't know what his game was, but she was too smart to be taken in by his faux charm. She needed a way out of Virginia, and that's all there was to it. Placing her helmet on the counter, she reached into her shoulder bag to pay.

The man said, "Your husband has already paid, ma'am, but I'd like to throw in a raincoat, as a wedding present." He pulled a slicker from a nearby rack.

Ian slapped his friend on the back. "The raincoat is a good idea, Dak, but I insist on paying for it. If you want to do something, just keep putting up the posters."

Cami snickered. "Posters? Is there a bounty on your head?"

Imitating the Godfather, Ian snarled. "You might want to think twice if you're planning on turning me in, missy. Are you sure you can operate the bike if I go to the slammer?"

Dak cackled. "Surely you know . . . your husband is a wanted man, Mrs. Benrey."

On the way out, Cami paused at a counter to admire an assortment of tiny bells inside the glass case. "How cute."

Ian said, "They're Guardian Bells, a sort of lucky charm that bikers attach to the bottom of their bikes."

"I love them."

"Then pick one and consider it a present. According to legend, your blessings are doubled if you receive a Guardian bell as a gift."

"Thanks, I will. I could sure use a double-dose of blessings."

Dak placed each bell on top of the counter. The decision wasn't an easy one, but Cami finally settled on the one with a cross.

She crawled on the back of the Harley without any prompting. "It's getting late. Do you ride in the dark?"

"Of course. Haven't you heard? Midnight bugs taste best."

"Yuk!" The only thing that kept her from jumping off while she still could, was the dreadful thought of going back home.

"Where are we going?"

"Does it matter?"

"Not really." Her tone softened. "Ian . . . I know you were trying to protect me, but I'm sorry you felt the need to lie for me."

"Did I lie?"

"You told Dak we were married." She quickly added, "Not that I'm reprimanding you, but I don't expect you to cover for me, if it requires lying. It's not right."

"I told him to call us the Benreys. I never said it was your name, nor did I say you were my wife."

"But you know what he thought. And that wasn't all. You said my name was Kimi."

"Wrong again. Maybe it was my Southern drawl. Dak's the one who kept calling you Kimi. Why didn't you correct him . . . tell him your name was Camille and you have a last name but it's not Benrey?"

"You're right. You weren't the only deceptive one. I could've easily corrected it." She paused. "Ironic, really."

"How's that?"

"Lies are the very reason I left home and now I'm becoming like the ones I'm running from. I like Dak. Call him tomorrow and tell him the truth."

"He knows."

"What? He knows who I am?"

"I doubt he knows who you are, but he knows who you aren't. He knows you aren't Mrs. Benrey."

"What makes you think he didn't believe you?"

"Number one reason, Dak knows me. He reads me like a book, and he knows the last thing I want in my life is a wife."

Camille couldn't explain why she felt offended, she only knew that she did. Why should it matter to her whether he ever wanted to get married? "You have something against women?"

"Hey, I love women. My mother was one. I'm just saying I'm not the marrying kind. Burned once, her fault. Burned twice, my fault. I got closer to the fire the second time than I ever will again."

"So, you're divorced?"

"No, no, no. Never been married."

"Then, I don't understand why you're so bitter."

"Who said I was bitter? I like to think of it as being informed."

Once they were on the road, Cami found her muscles relaxing, and to her surprise she enjoyed everything about the exhilarating ride. Who would've known it could be so much fun?

A couple of hours down the road, she yelled, "How much further before we stop?"

"There's a place about twenty miles from here, where we can stay the night, but if you need to stop sooner, I'll pull off at the next exit."

"No, I'm fine. Keep going. I'm sleepy, though."

"Then go to sleep."

"Are you insane? On the back of a motorcycle? No way."

Less than thirty minutes later, Camille jerked her head back and opened her eyes when the bike came to a halt in a wooded area. She glanced around. There were three RV's and a couple of tents set up in the grove of trees. She could see flickering lights from a small motel on the other side of the highway. "Is that the motel where we'll be spending the night?"

"Nope."

"Then why are we stopping?"

Ian pointed to a sign on a brick building in the woods. "Rest Rooms."

It made absolutely no sense why he would've stopped at the RV Park, when it wouldn't have taken two minutes longer to get checked into the nearby motel.

He jumped off and offered his hand to assist her.

On her way back from the Ladies restroom, she spotted Ian kneeling beside a tent, putting down stakes. "What are you doing?"

"Setting up the tent."

"But you said . . ."

"I said we aren't staying in the motel. I thought you understood."

"Well, I didn't. And I hope you don't think I'm spending the night in the woods."

"Don't be silly. You're much safer here with me than you were when you were standing on the highway, thumbing. We'll get a few hours' sleep and strike out again at first light. I've been riding since daybreak and I'm bushed. You'll find a sleeping bag in the tent"

"That's ridiculous. I can't take your tent and leave you to

sleep out here."

He smiled. "I'm flattered, but as tempting as it sounds, I couldn't possibly. I'm not that kinda guy."

"If you think I was suggesting . . ." She winced. "But I'm sure you know better." She slung her backpack over her shoulder. "You can have your tent and stay in the woods with the bears, but I plan to sleep in a bed—at the motel."

"I don't think you want to do that."

"Obviously, you don't know me." She spun away in a huff. "I'll be ready by the time you are in the morning."

"Have it your way, but I know that dump, and trust me, you'd be safer out here with the bears than inside the motel with a pack of wolves."

She got as far as the motel parking lot, when she heard cat whistles from three unsavory-looking characters. She turned to run, when she heard Ian chuckle.

He said, "Well, that didn't take as long as I expected."

"You followed me."

"Yes ma'am. Now, if you don't mind, I'm really tired. Even Guardian Angels have their limitations." He walked her back to the campsite, grumbling under his breath.

Her voice cracked. "You hate me, don't you?"

His jaw jutted forward. "Sheesh woman, If I hated you, I would've left you standing on the interstate. Don't make me sorry that I didn't."

Her lip quivered. "Why didn't you?"

"Look, I don't hate you, but I might learn to, if you don't get in the tent and go to sleep."

"No. I can't take your tent. I'll sleep outside."

"Suit yourself." He pulled out a large yellow poncho and threw it on the ground under a tree. "In case it rains," he mumbled.

"Rain? Really? You think it might?" When he ignored her, she pushed her backpack under her head and lay on the hard ground. Gazing up at the starless sky, she said, "Ian, what kind of posters were you and Dak talking about?"

"Aargh! What's with you, woman? You've had all day to ask questions. Would you please get in the tent and save the senseless chatter for another time? I'm exhausted."

"You don't have to be so grumpy, for crying out loud." It seemed rather silly for both of them to sleep in the open when there was a perfectly good tent set up. Especially, if rain was in the forecast. She stood, picked up her backpack and watched as Ian unstrapped his guitar case. He leaned against a tree and adjusted the strings.

"I thought you were tired."

"Playing relaxes me. Chatter doesn't." He pointed toward the tent. "Goodnight."

CHAPTER 3

Cami stretched out on the sleeping bag and marveled at how roomy it was on the inside of the tent. She could hear Ian strumming his guitar and singing some of her favorite tunes. He was good. Really good. She hummed along and soon found herself singing the familiar lyrics, until her eyelids closed for the last time.

Shortly after two a.m., a frightening clap of thunder, streaks of lightning, and the sound of heavy rain pounding against the canvas aroused her from a deep sleep. Ian's guitar was propped up in the corner of the tent. Peeking out through the flap, her throat tightened, seeing the poor guy hunched on the ground, a poncho his only protection from the drenching rain.. His arms were wrapped around his knees while his head rested on his knee caps.

How could she go back to sleep, while he sat on wet ground with nothing but a poncho to protect him from the downpour. "Get in here," she screamed, her voice almost drowned out by the thunderous storm.

Without looking up, he shouted. "I'm fine. Go to sleep."

"Now, who's being stubborn? It's lightening and there's room in here for both of us. Besides, I've already drawn a boundary line on the sleeping bag and promise not to cross it."

At that, he lifted his head and grinned. "Pinky promise?"

She held up her little finger. "Pinky promise. Hurry!"

He jumped up and rushed inside. Camille had the sleeping bag spread out across the ground. A bright red lipstick line was drawn all the way down the center. With tongue in cheek, she said, "Claudette Colbert had her Walls of Jericho, and I have my Red Sea."

He stretched out and closed his eyes. "I have no idea what you're talking about, but if it's all the same to you, we'll discuss it later."

"It was in the movie. There was only one room available, and Clark Gable and Claudette . . ." she stopped talking when she noticed he'd already dozed off.

The sun had barely risen over the horizon, when Ian shouted, "Wake up, sleepy woman. We need to hit the road."

Cami rolled over and caught him glaring. "What are you gawking at?"

He made a clicking sound with his tongue. "I trusted you. I'm serious. I did. You look like such a nice girl." He plunked his hands on his hips. "Well, you certainly can't tell a book by its cover."

She yawned. "I have no clue what you're babbling about."

"Looks like you crossed the Red Sea while I was sleeping."

She sat straight up and stretched. The preposterous suggestion made her snicker. "You're very arrogant if you think I harbored any such absurd thoughts."

"My eyes don't lie. What's that verse in the Bible? 'Be sure your sins will find you out?' Seems the Red Sea rubbed off when you huddled up to my side. Did you honestly think I wouldn't notice?"

She jumped up and twisted around. Her jaw dropped at the sight of a smeared red streak on the back of her shorts. "Oh m'goodness. I have no idea how that happened. I seldom move in my sleep."

He grinned. "I promise not to tell if you won't."

"Don't be silly. There's nothing to tell and you know it. I'm hungry. Where are we gonna eat breakfast?"

"The Pancake House in Pigeon Forge. It's only about forty miles from here."

"Forty miles! I'll be starved by that time. I'm sure there's somewhere closer."

"Maybe, but after riding for two days, I'm ready to get home. We'll leave as soon as I get a shower and change."

"Yeah, I'd like to do the same." She grabbed a fresh change of clothes and as they strolled down the path toward the Bath Houses,

Cami said, "I've never been to Pigeon Forge. What do you do there?"

"Never been? Well you're in for a treat. We get thousands of tourists who come to the mountains each year with their families, and it's my job to provide them with a clean place to come to.

"A janitor!"

"Call it what you will."

"I didn't mean to offend. I suppose you prefer maintenance engineer?"

"Label me any way you think appropriate, woman."

"I wish you wouldn't call me woman. I have a name."

Cami finished dressing and walked back to the campsite. "I'm starving, Ian. Why can't we eat at the first place we come to?"

He walked over to the bike and fumbled in a knapsack. "I think I have a stick of jerky in my bag that will tide you over."

"Ugh. No thanks."

"Then you aren't starving."

She groaned. "I think an evil spirit has taken over my Guardian Angel. What's so important about getting to Pigeon Forge?"

"I told you. It's where I work. Don't worry. You'll be on your own, once we're there and you can come and go as you please."

"You sound eager to get rid of me. If you recall, it was your idea to bring me along."

He hung his head. "You're right. Sorry if I sounded agitated.

Truth is, I didn't get much sleep last night between the rain and the Red Sea."

Cami's mouth watered at the sight of every restaurant billboard along the interstate. Never had forty miles seemed so long.

The Pancake House was packed, with people winding around the block. She moaned. "Yikes! It'll take forever to get fed. Surely, you knew it would be like this. Why don't we try the place across the street?"

He said, "Are you gonna nag this much after we're married?"

"Married? Ha! In your dreams."

"A nagging wife is not a dream, sweetheart, it's a nightmare." Ian drove around the block and parked the bike back of the Pancake House, then led her inside through the kitchen door.

"So this is where you work? Why didn't you say so?"

A large, gray haired woman stood in front of a grill and flipped a pancake.

Ian wrapped his arms as far as they'd go around the cook's thick waist. "Miss me, Maude?"

She plopped the pancake on a tall stack and handed the platter to a waiter. With a near-toothless grin, she stepped away from the griddle, turned, and threw her arms around Ian. "Been praying for you, son. You know how I worry when you're on the road."

"I know, Maude, and I love you for praying. Keep it up."

"Always." She stepped back up to the stove, picked up a large green bowl and poured puddles of batter onto the griddle. "Wish I had time to hear about your trip, but we're short of help this morning."

"Didn't mean to stop you. Just had to come see my girl."

A waitress walked in and squealed. "Ian Benrey! We missed you! I've just cleaned a table over in the corner. It's yours."

With something more disturbing than hunger on her mind, Cami forgot all about an empty stomach. Ian's words played over and over in her head. *Are you gonna nag this much after we're married?* The married part, though utterly preposterous, didn't bother her nearly as much as the nagging part—which she remorsefully conceded had a tad of truth in it. She bristled. If she nagged, it was his own fault. He could've told her that employees received backdoor privileges, which would've kept her from fretting about the long line. Was he still miffed at being referred to as a janitor? At least he had a job, which was more than he could say for her.

Cami took a seat and glanced around the crowded room. "Why didn't you . . . never mind."

"Go ahead. Whatever's on your mind, feel free to spit it out."

"It was nothing." She chose to let it go, rather than risk being a nag. "So this is where you work? Seems like a great crew to work with. They all appear to like you."

"So, what is it that surprises you most? Me being a janitor, or that people might actually like me?"

"If you're trying to make me feel like a heel, you've

succeeded, and I'm beginning to think that's your ultimate goal. There's nothing wrong with being a janitor, but you called me something worse."

"When?"

"You called me a nag."

"If I recall, I only asked if you intended to nag. I never said you were nagging."

"But we both know what you meant." They'd soon be parting ways, and it wouldn't feel right to leave with tension between them. There was no denying his good outweighed his bad. She considered all he'd done for her, when he could've left her standing on the highway. Looking back, she realized if she hadn't been so angry at the time, she would've known how stupid it was to be on the Interstate thumbing. The movie was made nearly eighty years ago, for crying out loud. She couldn't deny that from the beginning, Ian had placed her welfare ahead of his with very little thanks. Moisture filled her eyes as she murmured, "Shall we call a truce?"

He wrapped his hands around his coffee cup and sipped slowly while she waited for his answer. He picked up a napkin and wiped his mouth. His gaze locked with hers.

Her heart hammered.

He smiled, then gave a slight nod and held up a closed hand. "Fistbump!"

The ominous dark cloud that seemed to hover over them lifted and they were soon laughing. It was a slap-happy, silly sort of laughter when everything suddenly seems funny for no reason at all.

The meal was even more delicious than Cami had imagined and the hefty serving of blueberry pancakes and link sausage was too much food, even for a starving woman. When they finished eating, she asked for a to-go box.

Ian watched as she forked the leftovers into the Styrofoam box. "And I suppose you plan to eat cold pancakes for lunch?"

"Sounds like you're making fun of me, but I don't care. I figure they'll be good for breakfast in the morning." She swallowed hard, realizing she had no idea where she'd be when she ate her next breakfast.

He lowered his head. "I'm sorry if I sounded insensitive." He reached in his pocket for his wallet. "I have a little money. I can lend you whatever you need."

"Thank you, but I'm not broke. Not yet, but I plan to be frugal. I have enough to tide me over for a while, but I could sure use a job. Do you know if your boss is hiring? Your friend Maude said they're short of help. I've never flipped pancakes, but I'm a quick study."

Ian shook his head. "They have a waiting list, but Pigeon Forge is a good place to start looking for work. What can you do?"

She flinched. "Not much, I'm afraid."

"What were you doing before you took to the road?"

"I was a student at Virginia Tech and scheduled to finish next semester.

28

"Bummer! There must've been something terribly troubling to make you leave home, so close to reaching your goal. If you ever get ready to talk about it, I'm a good listener."

"Thanks. I'm not sure I'll ever be ready to talk about it. I want my past to stay in the past."

The waitress brought a box and Cami put two left-over pancakes inside, then forked a lone sausage link from Ian's plate. She reached across the table and placed her hand over his. "Thank you, Ian."

"For the sausage?"

"For everything. I was furious when I ran away and frankly didn't care what happened to me."

"That was obvious when I saw an immaculately dressed, beautiful young woman, all alone on the Interstate, pleading with a perfectly manicured thumb for someone . . . *anyone* to take her away."

A tear slipped down her cheek. "I realize now how foolish it was, but I was too distraught to think straight. You probably saved my life." She slid her chair back, picked up her box and stood. "I need to get my bag from your bike." She stretched her arms out for a hug. "Goodbye, my friend."

Ian jumped up. "Bye? Where do you think you're going?"

"Gotta look for a job. I agree, this town appears to be a great place to start. With so many restaurants, my chances are probably as good here as anywhere."

They reached the door and Ian said, "Wait." He stopped at a

gumball machine and put in a quarter. A blue gumball fell out and he handed it to Cami.

She popped it in her mouth and waited while he put in another quarter. A gold-tone ring with a fake pearl, fell out.

"Bingo!"

Cami giggled. "Aww, so sorry."

"Sorry? Are you kidding? I have gum. I needed a ring." He fell to his knees. "Camille Benrey, will you be my girl?"

She scanned the room with her eyes, then whispered. "Get up silly."

"I'm waiting for your answer."

"People are staring, Ian."

"Let them stare. I'm staying here until I get an answer."

"Yes, yes! I'll be your girl." She turned her head to hide her smile.

He stood, reached for her right hand and slid the ring on her long, slender finger. "Perfect."

CHAPTER 4

Standing outside the Pancake House, Cami said, "Okay, you're up to something, Ian Benrey. What's going on?"

"It may be a long shot, but I have an idea for a job if you're willing."

"Seriously? Hey, I'll try anything, legal or moral. What do you have in mind?"

"You have a nice voice, Cami. I can't promise anything, but would you be interested in singing?"

"You mean like with a tin cup, for tips?" She shook her head without allowing him to answer. "I know you mean well, Ian, and trust me, my goal is not to get rich, but I need to make enough money to at least afford a one-star motel. I'm afraid my singing wouldn't pull in enough tips for me to survive."

"I'm not talking tips. I'm talking a real job as a real

performer."

"Me? A performer? You can't be serious."

"Of course, I'm serious. I don't suppose you've ever done any acting?"

"I've never been in a big production, if that's what you mean. I did take five years of drama growing up and had the lead in several plays in Community Theatre. Then, there was the Drama Club in high school. But a real performer?" The smile left her lips and she shook her head. "Me sing? No, that's crazy."

"It's worth a shot. Surely, with a voice like yours, you've done some singing in your time."

"Voice like mine? When have you ever heard me sing?"

"Shortly before the Red Sea parted, I was playing the guitar and could hear you singing inside the tent. You have a mesmerizing voice."

As fascinating as it sounded, she quickly dismissed the crazy notion. "I appreciate the compliment, but I don't have the experience. I've sung a few solos at church and in the choral group at the University, but all I ever got were a few bouquets. Flowers don't pay rent, nor feed you when you're hungry. I know you want to help, Ian, but that's out of the question. I'm sure something will turn up. Again, thanks for everything. I need to get my backpack from your bike before you go. I'll start on this side of the street and apply at every store until someone hires me."

"And where do you intend to stay tonight?"

"I'll find a place. Please stop worrying, Ian. I'm not your

responsibility."

"What do you mean, you're not my responsibility. You're my girl, remember? You're wearing my ring."

She giggled. "And it's a beautiful ring." She twisted it on her finger. "I'll wear it forever."

"That's better. There's a campground back of a motel, and I know the manager. Most people bring their own RV's, but he usually has a couple of campers available. A little creek runs between the motel and the campground, and the ducks are fun to watch. Let's check and see if Tom has a vacant camper."

"Shouldn't I try to get a job first, before looking for a place to stay? How do I know what I can afford, if I don't know how much money I'll be making?"

"Don't sweat the small stuff. I'm hoping to get you a job working with me, but we need to get you settled before nightfall."

"Working with you? What about the waiting list?"

He smiled. "You talk a lot, woman."

They rode through the campground and Cami waited with the bike while Ian went inside to talk with the manager.

There were RV's of all makes and sizes, parked on the grounds. Ian was right. It looked like a fun place to stay. Each space had a concrete patio and friendly-looking people were grilling out, while kids played in the creek. A couple of little boys stood on the banks throwing bread to the ducks. Happy people meandered around the park, seemingly without a care in the world.

What would it feel like to exist in such utopia? All her life Cami walked on egg shells to keep from upsetting, Jacob Gorham, the brutal man she grew up believing to be her father. She knew Jacob was drunk and didn't mean to spill the beans the night she ran away, but she was almost relieved to discover the same blood didn't run through their veins. The thing that hurt most was learning the truth about her mother—the one person she'd always trusted. Now, there was no one she could trust. Ian was a super nice guy, but if she couldn't trust those she knew best, she wouldn't be so gullible as to think she could trust a virtual stranger.

Ian ran toward her with a broad smile while waving a paper in the air. "Tom had one left. We got it. It's a small travel trailer, but it's parked next to my RV. He's letting you have it rent free for thirty days. Says if you decide to stay in Pigeon Forge, he should have something nicer for rent at the end of the month."

"Thirty days, free? He must be a very good friend. Her gaze met his. "Wait . . . You did say it's next to yours, didn't you?"

"Yeah, I hope you didn't have the crazy notion I was gonna share my space with you, after that Red Sea thingy. I have a reputation to uphold, you know."

"Never crossed my mind. Why would you want to share quarters with a female who was only fairly good-looking?"

He cackled. "I was right. You *were* offended. For the record, though, I recall saying you were beautiful when I asked you to be my girl. Didn't that mean something?"

34

"Only if you meant it."

He drove through the campground and pulled up beside a small silver trailer that reminded her of a sardine box.

Ian said, "It's not much, I'll agree, but you'll have a bed and a roof over your head. Better than the tent, for sure. What d'ya say? Think you can call this home for a month?"

A month was beginning to sound like a very long time. If she were to guess the model, she'd guess 1940's. "It's very . . . uh . . . tiny, but I'm sure it was the cat's meow, back in its day. I wonder if Claudette Colbert ever stayed here." She assumed it was a joke until Ian reached in his pocket and proudly displayed a key.

His face twisted. "Hey, what's wrong? You don't want it?"

She feigned a smile. "It's . . . it's fine. Thanks."

"That's good, because everything is filled this time of year. We're lucky Tom was kind enough to let us have it. Let's go inside and check it out."

Cami glanced around at the outdated piece of junk, hoping her disappointment wasn't visible. Her closet at home was twice as large as the whole interior of this rusty tin can. The old sofa was threadbare, and the bathroom was hardly big enough to turn around in. No tub? She hated showers. But it was rent-free. Why wasn't she grateful? If not for Ian, she'd be sleeping on a park bench. Shame enveloped her.

"So what do you think?" he asked.

Her voice quaked as she scrambled for an answer that would neither be offensive or a lie. "It'll do just fine. Thank you."

"You aren't very convincing. Are you sure?"

"Positive."

"I need to head to work, but I'll be back a little after ten tonight. If you think of anything you need, I'll pick it up for you when I get in."

"Don't bother. I'll be counting sheep by ten o'clock."

Cami watched out the window as he walked across the lot and opened the door to a luxurious motor coach. Seriously? Until tonight, she'd never experienced envy for what someone else had, since she'd always been given anything her heart desired. It was easy to brag she wasn't materialistic when there was nothing left to want. Her stomach wrenched.

Eager to get a hot shower, she undressed and stepped into the tiny enclave. Stored up tears washed down her face. She pulled a tee shirt from her backpack and after dressing for bed, walked over to the window air-conditioner and tried to read the faded-out instructions glued to the top. A few minutes later, she sank down on the knotty old mattress and drifted off to sleep.

At ten-fifteen, a knock on the door caused Cami to sit straight up in bed. "Who's there?"

"Ian."

"I'm in bed, Ian and I'm fine. Don't need anything. See you in the morning."

"Let me in, Cami. I have exciting news. This won't wait."

"Hold on." She groped in the darkness, trying to find a wrap in the unfamiliar surroundings. "Ouch!" She jumped around on one foot after stumping her toe on a table leg. Grabbing an afghan from the sofa, she threw it around her shoulders and hobbled to the door. "Come on in." She muffled a yawn and hoped it wouldn't take long for him to say what he had to say. "What's going on?"

"You have a job interview in the morning at nine o'clock."

"Cool. What'll I be doing?"

"You'll be working with me. Be ready at eight-thirty. This is perfect. I could hardly wait to tell you."

Cami was glad he'd given up on the foolish idea of her trying to survive as a street singer. She needed a real job. "Minimum wage, I presume?" The minute the words slipped from her mouth, she felt like a heel. Why couldn't she share his enthusiasm. What did she expect, with no skills? "I didn't mean to sound ungrateful. I really appreciate it, Ian. Thank you. I'll be ready."

"Sorry to have disturbed your sleep, but I needed to make sure you could be ready in time. A pair of jeans and light jacket will be sufficient for the interview. No need to dress up."

After he left, Cami had trouble falling back to sleep. Random thoughts ran through her head. Would she be a waitress, a cashier, a hostess, or heaven forbid . . . a *cook*? But didn't Ian say she'd be working with him? A janitor! *Eeyew. Mopping and cleaning toilets?*

There were things she failed to consider when she decided to run away. Not that she regretted leaving, for she'd do it all over again for all the same reasons. But she did regret being so unprepared for life. She'd never touched a mop or toilet brush, and now it appeared they were about to become her tools of trade.

Her throat tightened. As much as she didn't want to admit it, she missed her mother. It didn't mean she wasn't angry as all get-out. She was. But Cami could've forgiven her for past transgressions, if only she'd been truthful. *Why Mom? Why did you lie to me?* She had a right to know her father, didn't she? Unanswered questions rolled around in her head so fast she couldn't keep track. Who was he? What was he like? Did she favor him?

Her imagination soared. Was she a love child, or conceived by a man who was no more than a ship passing through the night? How many men were in her mother's life? Did her father know he had a daughter?

CHAPTER 5

Ian knocked on Cami's door at eight-fifteen the next morning. "Excited?"

She nodded, then bit her lip. Truth was, the idea of becoming a custodian didn't excite her at all. Scared, yes. Excited, no. Until recently she'd never realized how easily one could lie without admitting it was a falsehood, but how could she confess to Ian she was terrified? Girls with far less education worked as servers, cooks and housekeepers. She was smart, so why did she feel so inadequate?

Ian pulled up to a beautiful yellow stone building, with a huge marquee with flashing lights. Recognizing a life-sized picture of Ian holding a guitar, she screamed. "Ian, who *are* you?"

"You know who I am. I never lied to you, Cami. I'm Ian Benrey." He grinned and pointed to the sign. "See? That's me.

Says so on the marquee."

She wailed. "You never lied? Of course, you did. You're just like everyone else in my life. All liars. I feel like such a fool." She sobbed while beating on his back with her fists. "I suppose you think it was funny, pretending to be a janitor, when you're a famous entertainer. Well, I don't." She bounded off the bike and ran down the sidewalk, bawling.

Ian drove slowly beside her. He yelled, "I never lied to you, Cami. I wouldn't lie to you. I can explain."

She stopped and wiped her wet face with the back of her hand. "Five seconds, then I never want to see you, again, Ian Benrey. You can tell all your fans what a joke you pulled on a gullible girl you picked up on the highway. That should make a funny story for one of your shows."

"Cami, stop and think about what I told you. I said I needed to get to Pigeon Forge because it's where I work, but I never said I worked at the Pancake House. I told you I wanted to eat there, not sweep the floor or wash dishes. You're the one who jumped to those conclusions without really listening to me. Then, last night, I told you I arranged for you to have an interview where I work, and that's exactly what I've done. Now, please tell me why you're calling me a liar."

"On the way to Pigeon Forge, I asked you what you did for a living. Why didn't you tell me you were an entertainer with your own show? Instead, you misled me by answering, 'I try to keep things clean.'"

"Exactly. And failing to allow me to finish, you immediately had me working as a janitor. If you'd waited, I would've explained, but I've learned you have a bad habit of forming your own conclusions, instead of listening to what's being said."

"It was a natural conclusion to draw and you know it, since keeping things clean has absolutely no relation to your being a bigshot star of your own show."

"Begging your pardon, but it has everything to do with my line of work. The entertainment industry today has reached gutter levels. I was attempting to explain my goal has been to work in a family friendly place, where people can bring their kids and expect to see a clean, wholesome show. I found a venue where I not only can keep things clean, it's an expectation." He glanced at his watch. "Now, can we please finish this discussion later? You have an interview coming up."

"Yeah? Doing what? I don't think there's room on that sign for two names."

He smiled. "Then we'll insist on a larger sign."

"I'm in no mood for jokes, Ian. You've had your fun. Now, I want to go back to the trailer, I'll take charge of my life from here on out."

"Really? Somehow, I thought you might be wanting something a little more comfortable than life in a sardine can. If you land this job, it's your way out."

Sardine can? Funny, he used the same words she thought of when she first saw the tiny trailer. He was right. She did want out.

All the things she'd said about not being materialistic, now seemed a bit ludicrous. She was a tad more materialistic than she'd wanted to admit. "Fine. I'll go in. But at least tell me what I'm interviewing for."

"Backup singer to begin with and who knows after that? You could soon have your own show."

She stopped in her tracks. "Sing? You have to be kidding. I can't sing. Well, not well enough to be someone's backup."

"Sure, you can. I've heard you singing and you're good. You're real good. Now, stop dragging your feet. I promised to have you here by nine o'clock."

"But look at me. I'm not dressed for an interview. I thought I was . . . "

"You thought you'd be scrubbing floors at the Pancake House. I know. But don't worry about how you're dressed. You're fine." He winked. "I think you're fairly nice-looking. At least you are when you smile."

She attempted a smile, albeit a weak one. "I haven't practiced, Ian. I don't even have music. What will I sing?"

"I Can Only Imagine."

"I'm glad you can. I wish I could." She shook her head emphatically. "No. Absolutely not. I can't possibly go in there. I'd embarrass both of us. I have no idea what to sing, and my mind is a total blank."

"Weren't you listening? I said you'll be singing, 'I Can Only Imagine."

"You mean like the song in the movie?"

"Exactly like the song in the movie. The same song you sang in the tent the night you crossed the Red Sea."

"You'll never let me live it down, will you?" Her smile faded. "You really think I can do it?"

"I know you can. We'll have a chance to go over it a couple of times together, then the third time, you're on your own." He walked her into the building. "Scared?"

"Terrified."

Cami came out of the sound booth and jumped into Ian's arms. "We did it," she squealed.

"No, you did it, babe. You sounded awesome. Ralph was very impressed. I promised him he would be. You've got quite a voice."

Cami wasn't sure if he initiated the kiss or if she did, but it was a kiss she'd dream about for the rest of her life. She instinctively knew there'd be many more, but none could ever match that first breathtaking, heart stopping, skin tingling kiss.

Two months later, they ran out of a Sevierville Wedding Chapel, as Mr. and Mrs. Ian Benrey.

CHAPTER 6

Two years later . . .

Camille opened her eyes and flailed her arm to the other side of the bed. Empty! As empty as her bed had been for over eighteen long, lonely months . . . until last night. She rolled over and grabbed the pillow beside her head and sniffed. Her throat tightened. She could still feel his breath warming her neck, his lips caressing hers. Clutching the pillow tightly, she inhaled again and sucked in his scent. *A dream?* No. It was real. Had to be. "Yes, you *were* here, weren't you babe?"

Questions whirled in her head, though it was useless to dwell on the how's and whys, since there was no possible earthly explanation for what took place after she went to bed. But what if it wasn't earthly—but heaven-sent? Why not? How many times had she heard folks say, 'God works in mysterious ways.' If what happened last night wasn't mysterious, Cami couldn't imagine what sort of event could possibly fall under the category.

Countless times since Ian's death, she'd groaned and even cried aloud, "God, it isn't fair. He was too young to die. If only I could have one more night . . .just one more night with him." And then it happened.

After enduring eighteen months of unbearable grief, she was convinced God had seen her tears and had given her what she asked for—*One more night*. Doesn't the Bible say Hezekiah's prayer was answered, because God heard his prayer and saw his tears? Renewed faith, hope and love arose from a dark pit deep within her heart and flowed like hot lava gushing from a huge volcano.

She bounced into the kitchen and greeted her housemate, Rydetha, affectionately known as Deedee—a sweet but opinionated woman forty years Cami's senior.

"You're up bright and early, sugar. Sit down at the table. Breakfast is almost done." Barely five-feet tall, the jovial woman who referred to herself as "fluffy," lovingly hovered over Cami, treating her like the daughter she never had. "I scrambled a couple of eggs and fried a sausage patty for you, hon. The butcher got a tad too much pepper in the sausage for my taste, but it should suit you fine. I don't know how you tolerate spicy food, the way you do. Toast is in the toaster."

Cami shook her head. "Thanks, but I'm not hungry. Maybe later. I'll just have a cup of coffee for now." She picked up the morning paper from off the table and skimmed over the headlines.

"Cami, you can't stop eating again. It ain't healthy sugar."

"Can't eat a thing. Too excited, Deedee. You won't believe what . . . never mind. I couldn't explain it if I tried."

Rydetha's eyes squinted. "Well, glory be. I thought there was something different about you when you walked into the kitchen. Who is this bubbly creature sitting at my table and what did you do with my despondent little Cami?"

Cami laid the newspaper down, reached across the table, grasped Rydetha's hand and squeezed tightly. Her voice came out in a low, coarse whisper. "I don't know if I should tell you, but I really want to."

"Tell me what honey? You know there's nothing you can't tell me, and from the look on your face, I'd say it's too good to keep bottled up, whatever it is."

Cami pulled back and clasped her hands together under her chin. "Okay but get ready for a shocker. You're not gonna believe this."

"Get on with it, sugar. You done got my curiosity up. I can't stand the suspense."

Leaning in, and speaking in a barely audible voice, Cami said, "Deedee, I saw him last night. I really did, and it was wonderful."

"Oh m'goodness, honey. Are you serious?" Her broad smile stretched across her rosy cheeks, causing her eyes to squint into tiny slits. With her elbows planted on the table, she gushed, "I'm so proud for you, darling."

"Really? I was afraid you'd think I was making it up."

"Well, I'll have to admit, after watching you grieve this long, it took me by surprise, but it's not as if I didn't believe it could one day happen."

"Well, I never dreamed it could happen."

"Stop dawdling, girl and tell me. I want to hear everything!"

Cami grinned. "Well, I may not tell you *everything,* but trust me, it was fine." She thrust her hand over her heart and swooned. "So fine."

Rydetha waved an arm in the air. "Praise the Lord. Hon, this is an answer to my prayers."

"Are you serious? You prayed for him to come into my life? That's awesome, Deedee. Thank you. I'm amazed that you have no reservations about praying for the impossible."

"Shug, the Bible tells us there's nothing impossible with God, and I take the Lord at His word."

"That's wonderful. I wish my faith was as strong as yours, You really *do* believe in miracles, don't you?"

"Yes ma'am, I certainly do. Oh, shug, hold on for about five seconds." She jumped up from the table. "I've waited this long, I reckon I can hold out a few more seconds. I don't want you to start telling it until I pour myself a cup of coffee, and then I want to sit and hear every last detail. You don't know how I've longed to see your eyes light up like this. It ain't nothing short of a miracle."

"Exactly. A miracle."

Deedee sat down with her coffee. "Okay, I'm ready now. Get on with it."

"It was incredible and I'm sure many others wouldn't believe it could happen, so it makes me happy, Deedee, to know that you not only believe me but that you prayed for it to happen." She grabbed Rydetha's hand and squeezed tightly. "Oh, Deedee, it was surreal. I didn't want the night to end."

Rydetha blew into her coffee cup. "Well, come on, girl . . . Who is he?"

Cami's brow furrowed. "Who? What do you mean, *who*? Ian, of course."

Rydetha's smile was quickly replaced with a look of horror. "*Ian?* Oh, Cami, I thought you were saying . . . I thought you had met . . . Oh m'goodness, shug, I didn't realize you were talking about a dream."

"But it wasn't a dream. Ian came back last night, just like you prayed. Don't you see, Deedee? Your prayer was answered and there's no way I can thank you enough. Of course, I prayed too, pleading for one more night, but the truth is, I never prayed, believing it could really happen. That's why I'm thinking now, it must've been your prayers that God answered."

"Oh, Cami, Cami, sweetheart . . . Ian isn't . . . Ian isn't with us anymore." Panic painted her face. She reached her hand across the table and gently placed it on Cami's arm. "You do know that, don't you, precious?"

Her jaw jutted forward. "Of course, I do. No one knows it better than I. I've missed him every hour of every day since he rode away."

Rydetha's chest swelled when she sucked in a lungful of air. Her eyes glistened with moisture. "Hon, my prayer wasn't for God to bring Ian back but for Him to heal your broken heart."

"Well, there you go. Proof that God answered your prayer. The only way my heart could've begun to heal would've been to see my darling Ian again and God allowed it to happen last night. Ian was in my bed."

Deedee teared up. "No, honey. No. No. No."

"Deedee, I know it sounds crazy, but I'm telling you Ian was here. He came back. He did. I was sound asleep, but I woke up when he crawled into our bed. He caressed my cheek with the back of his hand, just the way he used to do, then he took me in his arms and held me several minutes with neither of us saying a word. I was afraid if I spoke, he'd be gone. I sensed he'd have to leave again, but I chose to savor every moment we had together."

Rydetha picked up a napkin and dabbed at her eyes. "Honey, stop it. Ian is dead. You're hallucinating. I'd hoped in time you'd get better, but it's been going on too long. You need to make an appointment with Dr. Register. She can help you."

"The shrink? I'm not crazy, Rydetha." Her chin quivered. "You think I don't know he's dead? Trust me, no one knows better than I, but I heard a preacher once say that God speaks through various ways."

"That's true, honey, but I didn't hear you say you heard from God. Seems to me you said your deceased husband came into your bedroom in the middle of the night. Do you not understand that such an assertion sounds more than a little weird?"

Cami felt a knot in the pit of her stomach. What had she done? "I shouldn't have told you, but I was so excited and I thought of all people, you'd be the one who would understand."

"Think about what you're asking me to believe, Cami. You're saying a dead man entered your room last night and crawled in the bed with you. Honey, if a man was in your bed, we need to change the locks on the door, because there's one thing for sure—it was an intruder—and not your deceased husband." She pressed her lips together. "I don't mean to sound callous, because I really want to help you. But tell me why you thought Ian came into your room."

"I didn't *think* it—and I wasn't hallucinating. I'm telling you, I could feel him, smell him, see him. He was *here*. In this house. In my room. In my bed. I'm not asking you to believe it, but I know what happened and I have no reason to lie about it."

Rydetha swiped her wet cheek with the back of her hand. She pushed her chair back, walked around the table and wrapped her arms around Cami. "Honey, I'm sorry if I hurt your feelings. I don't pretend to know all God's ways, but I don't doubt He could've allowed you to experience a wonderful dream, to give your broken heart a much-needed rest. And for that, we should be thankful. You've hurt so long, Cami, and I can't tell you how refreshing it was to see you smiling this morning."

"No!" Her mouth flew open. "You don't get it. You still think I dreamed it. Deedee, he was real. As real as you are, standing here. I kissed him passionately, held him against me, felt his arms drawing me close. It was a very intimate experience that could never, ever have been duplicated in a dream. I'm telling you, my husband was in my bed."

"Okay, honey, I hear you. But you said you didn't talk to him, right?"

"Oh, but I did. You misunderstood. I said when he first crawled into bed, neither of us said anything. We simply reveled in the moment. After the initial shock wore off, we talked and talked until shortly before dawn, when he had to leave. I'm surprised you didn't hear us giggling. He thought it was hilarious that I still wear the ring he got out of the gumball machine at the Pancake House. He told me he'd planned to buy me a real pearl ring to replace it, but I reminded him that I didn't want another ring." She twisted it on her finger. "This ring might not be worth the quarter he plunked into the machine, but it's priceless to me. I won't ever take it off."

Rydetha sat with her face buried in her hands. She mumbled, "I don't know what else to say."

Cami glanced at her watch and jumped up. "Wow, it's later than I thought. If I don't hurry, I'll be late for class. Hard to believe I only have three more hours before I get my degree." She grabbed a piece of toast when she passed by the toaster.

Rydetha walked her to the door. "I hope you'll drive slow. The snow is melting, but I heard on the news there's been several accidents already this morning, due to the black ice."

"I'll be careful. And don't worry about me, Deedee. I know you don't understand, but I don't hold it against you. Honest."

"I know, honey. Don't forget about the black ice."

"I won't." She started down to the garage, then turned back. "Oh, Deedee, did I tell you Dr. Otis called her friend, Dr. Cunningham in Mobile and recommended me for a job?"

"Only a dozen times." She winked. "Just teasing you. I don't blame you for being excited, hon, although I get a little teary-eyed at the thought of you leaving me. Now you get on out of here. You don't need to be late for class and I don't want you driving fast to get there on time."

"I'm going. If I'm lucky enough to get that job in Mobile, I'll miss you for sure, Deedee, but how awesome will that be, if I can start my career by working with the famous Dr. Carlos Cunningham, a world renown cardiologist?"

"Honey, do you really think you're ready to take on such a responsibility?"

"Ready? I have a 4.0. Why wouldn't I be ready?"

"Forgive me, Cami, but I'm reminded of the proverb, 'Physician, heal thyself.'"

"What's that got to do with me?"

"You're not well, sweetie. Seems to me a healing needs to take place in your own life before you can be of benefit to others. I'm so worried about you, Cami. We need to get you help."

Cami rolled her eyes. "Bye, Deedee."

CHAPTER 7

February 13

Cami waltzed into the kitchen singing an age-old song that Rydetha hadn't heard since her church did away with their hymn books. How she missed the old ways. She joined Cami on the chorus. *Love Lifted Me. Love Lifted me. When nothing else could help, Love lift-ed me.* Rydetha dried her hands on a dish towel. "You're sounding mighty chipper this morning, sweetie."

"I love the words to that song, don't you, Deedie? *When nothing else could help, love lifted me?* That's how I feel. Like I'm floating on air."

Well, my, my! You sound as if you've had a Kumbaya experience."

Cami giggled. "Oh, m'goodness, that's funny. I hadn't thought of singing Kumbaya in a very long time—brings back memories of all the hugging and crying by the campfire that took place every year on the last night of youth camp. I'll admit, at fifteen, the love we shared was a sweet experience, though, sadly, it often faded after we returned home. Now, I ask myself, was it real? I thought so at the time." Her voice took on a more subdued tone. "I pray with all my heart that this fabulous feeling of euphoria never fades."

Sucking in a deep breath, Deedee asked a question for which she hoped would produce a sensible answer. "So, what has you in such a fabulous mood? Did you get your test grade back, yesterday?" Perhaps she shouldn't have said anything. But keeping her mouth shut was not one of Deedie's talents. Cami appeared to be doing much better lately, but could she be sure?

"I did, and I aced it, but it has nothing to do with school. You won't want to hear it. . ."

Rydetha stiffened.

Cami blew out a puff of air. "Okay, I might as well tell you. I'm sure you've guessed already." Her eyes twinkled. "He came last night."

Rydetha's flattened voice underscored her exasperation. "I suppose you're referring to your deceased husband?"

"Oh, Deedee, please don't refer to him that way. He has a name."

"Sorry. So, you *are* talking about Ian?"

She nodded. "It's been weeks. I wasn't expecting him, but he couldn't have come at a better time. I really needed him. I'd been so blue all day. Not an hour goes by that I don't think about him, but yesterday was especially hard."

"I suppose it had something to do with Valentine's Day approaching. Am I right?"

"Exactly. I was so sad, yesterday, seeing all the love stories on social media and television. I literally cried myself to sleep."

"I'm so sorry, honey. I saw the movies and ads, too, and I worried about you. I know you miss Ian, terribly."

"I do, Deedee, but you can't imagine how it has helped, just to be able to see him, even for brief intervals. He looks great. There's not a scratch on him. Isn't that amazing? I would've thought—"

Rydetha tuned her out, unable to sit by and listen to such nonsense. Her broken heart suffered in muted agony for her precious, emotionally-drained friend, although there were times she wanted to scream, *"Think, Cami! Think how stupid you're sounding."* Rydetha's motions rocked from anger to pity and back to anger. At times, she felt Cami was headed toward a mentally-deranged state, and it was her own doings. This pretense that Ian Benrey returned from the dead in the middle of the night couldn't continue. Somehow, someway, Rydetha had to reach her sweet young friend, before she became unreachable. She'd tried logic, hoping Cami would face reality and admit that as much as she desired it to be so—as much as she pretended it to be true—her husband had never, nor could he ever, return to her. Logic failed.

There was only one other option—an option Rydetha had resisted until now. As difficult as it was, she'd try listening. Instead of going into panic mode, as she had in the past, she'd play along and hope by allowing Cami to talk it out, she'd come to understand she needed help.

She cleared her throat, and in a sympathetic-sounding voice Rydetha hardly recognized as her own, said, "Had you already gone to bed when he arrived, sweetheart, or were you still up, studying?"

Cami's head cocked to the side, and her lip curled at the corner. "Seriously? I was beginning to think you were agitated—that you didn't care. You're serious? You're interested, really?"

"Yes, really."

"But I thought—"

Rydetha nodded. "I know what you thought, and you had every right. I refused to listen to you, didn't I? I was wrong, but it was such a shock when you first told me. You can understand that, can't you, sweetie?"

"I do understand, but it wasn't so much that you didn't listen, Deedee. What hurt the most was that you thought I was lying."

"Oh, no, honey. I never thought that. I believed that you believed it. It's just that I didn't believe it." She winked. "I hope you followed that, because I'm not sure I did."

Cami smiled. "I think I got it. So are you saying you're now ready to believe?"

She paused. "I've never doubted you, Cami. If you don't mind talking about it, I'm interested in hearing."

Her face lit up like a full moon, and Rydetha tried to ignore the stabbing pangs of guilt that made her feel like a conspirator.

Cami covered her smile with her hand. "You understand that I can't tell you everything. Some things are personal, between husband and wife."

"I understand."

"Well, last night was awesome. Let's see . . . you asked if I was still studying. No, I went to bed around eleven thirty, and I may have drifted off to sleep. I'm not sure. You know what I mean? Like you're dozing, in and out, half-asleep, half-awake?"

"Yes, I get it. Go on."

I couldn't have been asleep long, even if I was asleep, and I'm really not sure if I was or not. But I said that, didn't I?

Deedee nodded. "You did."

"Well, shortly after midnight—that's how I know that even if I'd already gone to sleep, it wasn't a deep sleep since I didn't go to bed until after eleven-thirty. I seldom fall asleep that quickly."

Deedee bit her lip. "Okay, so what happened shortly after midnight?"

"Thank you, Deedee."

"For what?"

"For being interested. I've needed to talk."

She felt a pang in her stomach. "Don't thank me, hon. Just go ahead and talk all you want to."

"As I was saying—"

"No need to repeat. Just start from midnight."

"Okay. I smelled his cologne before I even opened my eyes.

Somehow, I knew he was in the room. It seems it would've shocked me, but it didn't. Just like the last time, it felt so right. I called his name and then realized he was already in the bed. I suppose maybe I was asleep, now that I think about it, because I didn't hear him when he crawled in the bed. Anyhow . . . when I said his name, he slid over to my side of the bed." She snickered. "I'll spare you the romantic details, but after being together for an hour or so, he said he had something to show me. He jumped up, pulled me from the bed and told me he wanted me to go to the basement with him."

Rydetha's throat tightened. These hallucinations were even more serious than she realized. "Wow. So did you go with him downstairs?"

"Yeah. He walked over and lifted the canvas cover off the most beautiful pink and black Harley Softail I've ever seen. I flipped. It's awesome, Deedee. I can't wait to show it to you. He kissed me and said, 'Happy Valentine's Day, sweetheart.' So, what I perceived to be a very sad day, has become the best Valentine's Day of my life."

Rydetha chewed the inside of her cheek. "He gave you a motorcycle for Valentine's Day, and it was in the basement with a canvas cover on it. Is that what you're saying?"

"Yes. A gorgeous pink and black Harley Softail."

"And then you woke up and he was gone? Is that how it happened?"

"Well, no. You make it sound as if I dreamed it."

"Sorry. My bad. Naturally you had to go back upstairs, right?"

"Right. Ian walked me back up to the bedroom, tucked me in and kissed me one last time. He said, 'Hang tight, babe and remember to live right, play hard and love long.' I knew it was time for him to go, because that's what he'd always say before leaving me—even if he'd only be gone for a short while." Her lip trembled as she repeated his words. 'Live right . . . play hard . . . love long.' "I made him a promise I'd do it for him. Deedee, the truth is, I haven't been living right since I lost him."

"Oh, Cami, you're one of the sweetest people I know. If anyone lives right, it's you."

"I appreciate the kind words, but you were the one who told me the Bible says to think on those things that are good and not dwell on the bad."

"Yes, I did."

"I haven't been doing that, Deedee. Instead of being thankful for what I have and dwelling on the good times Ian and I had together, I was bitter for what I'd lost. All my thoughts have been consumed with anger and heartbreak."

"So, he said live right . . .and what was the other thing he asked of you?"

"Play hard."

"Oh, my. I haven't seen you in a playful mood since . . ."

"Since the day Ian rode away. I know."

"It would be good to see you enjoying life again. Do you think you're ready for that?"

"I am, Deedee. For Ian's sake. When he was alive, we truly played hard. We had so much fun together. We could laugh at the silliest things. But you're right—when he left, I stopped playing. I chose mourning over joy."

"Honey, you can't imagine how my heart is blessed, hearing this come from your lips. I don't have to tell you, I've been very concerned, seeing you drawing deeper and deeper into a shell." Deedee wanted to add that she'd feel much better when the frightening hallucinations would end, but she knew Cami wasn't ready to hear it. Patience was a virtue Deedee never professed to possess.

Cami's eyes veered away, as she muttered Ian's words, 'Live right, play hard and love long.' It was all he asked of me. The last one will be easy. "I'll love Ian Benrey forever and ever."

The conversation had gone even better than Deedee had imagined. Cami appeared ready to embrace reality, but it was vital that Deedee choose her words very carefully, for fear of alienating her. "Honey, about that bike you said Ian showed you last night. I don't want to upset you. I simply want to help you consider something you may not have thought of. You do remember Ian ordered a bike for you in December, before he died, don't you?"

"Of course, I remember. It was delivered with a dark green canvas cover and a big red bow."

"That's right. It's in the basement. And you refused to look at it. Am I right?"

"I couldn't, Deedee. I knew what it was, and I couldn't bear the thought of ever riding again, without Ian by my side."

"Now, why don't we go to the basement and see if the bike's still covered, the way it was when it was first delivered—and the way it still was, before you went to sleep."

"It is. I'm sure of it."

Deedee's throat tightened. She spoke in a slow, steady voice, hoping it would be neither intimidating or irritating. "Tell me if I get this wrong. You went to sleep last night, feeling sad at the thought of being alone with such a romantic holiday coming up. Pictures of lovers have been all over television and in the newspapers. You were lonely."

"Exactly."

"I understand, sweetie. Honest, I do. You fell asleep with a terrible yearning to be with the love of your life on such a romantic holiday."

"But, Deedee, you still believe—"

"Wait. Let me finish, and then you can help me understand in which areas I'm wrong. Last night, Ian came and you went with him to the basement."

"Yes."

"But it's very dark in the basement in daylight, and you do remember the bulb down there is burned out. It's pitch-black dark at night. How did you see to get down the stairs?"

"Well, I suppose . . ." she threw up her hands. "Maybe there's a short in the wiring. The light must've come on, because I could definitely see."

"Okay, so Ian showed you a bike and told you it was a Valentine's gift. But we know there's been a bike in the basement since December was a year ago. So, unless there are two bikes down there, you must've dreamed one of them." She paused. So far, so good. There were no tears, no outbursts. Deedee licked her dry lips. Perhaps it was time to zone in. "Dreams can seem very real, can't they, honey?"

"I know it sounds crazy, Deedee, but it was *not* a dream, True, Ian ordered the bike for my Christmas present the year he died, but he decided we'd call it a Valentine's present, since I had not unwrapped it. He was very sweet and said he understood why I couldn't bring myself to look at it previously, but last night he pulled off the cover, to show it to me, and oh m'goodness, Deedee, it's the most beautiful motorcycle I've ever seen. Ian said he chose pink because he remembered it was my favorite color. He was so pleased that I liked it. Before we went back upstairs, he placed the cover back on it, with the red bow still attached."

Rydetha's attempt at using psychology had been a pathetic failure. Why could Cami not understand how ridiculous it was to continue with these preposterous fantasies? "Let me get this straight, Cami. You're saying you got out of bed last night, walked with a ghost downstairs, he pulled the cover off the bike and then replaced it before you two ascended the stairs. You went back to bed and by morning, he'd vanished. How does that sound to you?"

"About right." The word ghost made Cami cringe. He was no ghost, but why argue? It was pointless and would only serve to drive a wedge between her and Deedee. Besides . . . if a woman had told her that her deceased husband came back for a visit and then mysteriously left again, would she have believed it? Maybe now . . . but certainly she would've scoffed at such an absurd allegation not so long ago.

Did it really matter if Rydetha or anyone else believed it? Ian came back, and she could only hope it would not be the last time.

CHAPTER 8

May 3rd

Rydetha squealed. "Oh my lands, Cami, you can't be serious. It's a death wish, isn't it?"

"That's ridiculous. I'm not afraid to die, Deedee, but you have it all wrong. This is something I must do. I promised Ian I'd do it, and he said he was proud of me. Called me a trooper. I'm determined to do this for my sweet husband."

"For Ian? Forgive me for being so blunt, Cami, but I've talked 'til I'm blue in the face. As difficult as it may be for you to accept, it's expedient for the sake of your mental health that you stop this nonsense and face reality. Ian is dead, honey and those fantasies you speak of, when you claim to see Ian are nothing more than that. Fantasies. If Ian really loved you—and I know he did—do you honestly think he'd want you to die the same way he did? I can tell you, the answer is 'no. Oh, honey, I hate to sound like a nag, but why can't you get it through your head that for you to strike out on such a dangerous trek on a motorcycle is nothing short of suicide?"

Camille smiled, determined not to argue. "I know you're concerned about me, Deedee, and I appreciate the fact that you care. I just wish I could do something to ease your mind."

"If you really mean that, you'll drive your car to Mobile. You have a perfectly good car, sitting in the garage, and it's a much safer way to travel. The notion of riding that *thing* from Tennessee to Alabama would be absurd, even if you'd been riding motorcycles for years—and you haven't."

She grinned. "Past tense."

"Pardon?"

"I *had* a good car. Sold it yesterday."

Rydetha's jaw dropped. "Oh, my lands, please tell me you didn't. What were you thinking, hon? What if a storm should come?"

"I've been caught in storms with Ian, plenty of times. No big deal. He says if you don't ride in the rain—you don't ride."

"Not 'says,' honey, but *said.* You're still speaking of him in the present. Ian *said.*"

"That's what I meant. But I'll find a place to pull off if the weather gets rough and wait for it to pass. Ian says . . . uh, Ian *said* that riding a motorcycle is only ten percent hands and feet and ninety percent eyes and mind. It's all about staying focused, and that I can do."

"Regardless, I can't help worrying."

"I know, but sometimes you spend far too much time conjuring up frightful scenarios that aren't likely to happen. Try being excited for me. The job sounds perfect and I'd love being close to the beach. Dr. Cunningham said I came highly recommended. I'm not worried about the bike ride, but I'm terrified that I might mess up the chance of a lifetime."

"I *am* happy that you're getting the interview, hon. I know how much you want the job, but if the hospital should hire you, can you imagine how disheveled you'll be by the time you get to work every morning? You have beautiful hair—and I'm sorry if I sound mean—but you look like Apple Annie when you pull off that helmet."

Camille cackled. "Did you say Apple Annie?"

"You wouldn't understand. It was an old Clark Gable movie."

"Nothing you can say will change my mind, Deedee." With her finger in the air, she pretended to write: "Note to self: Rent movie." She headed toward her room to finish dressing for the trip, but Rydetha—not ready to give up—followed close on her heels, pleading.

Camille yanked on the leather chaps, tucked in her shirt, pulled on a pair of leather boots, then zipped up her favorite gear . . . the vent jacket. She walked over to the full-length mirror and cocked her head. "How do I look?"

Rydetha groaned. "Like you're preparing for a funeral.

Yours."

She smiled and wrapped her arms around her best friend. "I don't anticipate anything happening to me on this trip, Deedee, but even if it should, please accept it as God's timing for me. Trust me, I'd be okay with that."

Rydetha's voice quaked. "You're scaring me, sweetie. Please, please, don't do this."

"I'm not scaring you. You're scaring yourself with these vain imaginations. Now, help me roll these clothes tight enough to fit into two saddle bags." Camille opened the bureau drawers and pulled out underwear, pj's, and two tee shirts, then tossed them on the bed.

Rydetha threw up her hands. "I wish there was a way to stop you, but I see I'm not getting through to you. I love you kid and I'll be on my knees praying until I get a call telling me you're on the other side of the mountain."

Camille snickered. "Your knees are gonna be sore, because I have no intention of rushing this trip . . . but I appreciate the prayers."

"Just promise to call as soon as you ride out of Death's Gap."

"Deals Gap. It's called Deals Gap and you know it."

"Cami, you're so focused on the ride, I'm not sure you're concentrating on *why* you're going. I don't want to nag, but honey, you can't wear jeans with holes in the knees, a ridiculous durag on your head and expect to get hired." Rydetha stomped over to Camille's closet and picked out two packable dresses, a pair of khaki pants, heels and a pair of sandals. She pulled out a fancy red frock that Camille hadn't worn since before Ian died. "You should take this, hon. You never know when you might need a nice dinner dress after you get there."

"I'm quite sure I won't. Ian says saddlebags may not hold everything I want, but they'll hold everything I need. I'm sure a dinner dress is something I can do without."

"Well, even with your looks, you aren't likely to win the attention of an attractive young doctor, dressed in tacky jeans and a durag."

"You don't give up, do you, Deedee? How many times must I remind you, I'm not interested in attracting a man? Neither a doctor, a cook, a lawyer nor a ditch-digger. I had the best, and he's gone. I'll never marry again. Never!"

"Cami, I know you think there'll never be another love in your life, but you're young, beautiful and extremely intelligent. Sweetie, you're destined to be sought out by many desirable young men after you get to Mobile. All I ask is that you keep an open mind."

"Destined? The only thing I'm destined for, is to live out my life as Ian Benrey's widow, and I'm good with that. I wish you could accept it. Frankly, I don't believe in destiny, but I do believe that true love comes only once in a lifetime and it's up to the individual to find it. I found mine. I'm done. I'd rather die of old age as Ian Benrey's widow than to live out a long, boring life rocking on a front porch with some paunchy, old, toothless geezer that I could never love."

Rydetha's chin quivered. "I'm terrified that your chance for a long life could be snuffed out before you get on the other side of the mountain."

Camille wrapped her arms around her friend. "I know you worry about me, Deedee, and I do appreciate your concern, but this ride is something I must do."

"What if that monstrous vehicle falls over?"

"If I have to lay it down, I'll pick it up."

"Have you ever picked one up?"

She grinned. "No. Ian showed me what to do, but his bike was much larger. I'm sure I can handle this one, though. It's a lot lighter than the older models." Her eyes glistened as she watched Rydetha roll a little black dress. "Thanks for helping me pack. That dress is Ian's favorite."

"Not *is*, hon. *Was*."

Camille had learned to ignore the sarcasm. "Did I ever tell you I married in that dress?" Not waiting for an answer, she continued. "It's true. Ian asked me to wear it the day we got married in the Chapel. Can you believe it?" The corner of her lip lifted in a slight smile. "I told him brides don't marry in black—but he called it silly. Maybe it was, but I wanted to look pretty for him, so I gave in." She scratched her head. "Deedee, I've never thought about it until now . . . but do you suppose that was an omen?"

"An omen? A dress?"

"Yeah. You know . . . of what was to come? A sign that death would soon separate us? I don't think people hold to it much anymore, but isn't black the customary color to wear to funerals?"

"Cami, I Suwannee, you swat at a gnat while swallowing a camel."

She cackled. "Say, *what*?"

"I'm just saying you make light of perilous situations that should scare the heebee-jeebies out of you, while fretting over the frivolous."

Camille snickered. "I'm not sure what you just said, Deedee, but I'm guessing your answer is, 'Nope, not an omen.'"

"That's precisely what I'm saying. A black dress had nothing to do with what happened to your husband, for crying out loud, but I can tell you what did. It was a motorcycle, whizzing in and out between cars, on an eleven-mile stretch of highway that has 135 treacherous hairpin curves. That's what took him from you. Honey, I know everything I'm saying is going in one ear and out the other, but if you aren't going to pay attention to me, stop and think what Ian would say to this crazy stunt you're planning. Do you honestly think he'd encourage you to try something that even he couldn't perfect?"

"I know exactly what he'd say, because he's already said it. Six weeks and four days ago, when he last came back, we discussed the wreck. I told him I hated that stretch of dangerous highway for claiming his life, and I won't ever forget his stunned expression. With his hands cupped around my face, he said, 'Sweetheart, the Tail of the Dragon didn't take my life . . . a drunk driver did.'"

He said, "He cut me off and it could've happened anywhere, even on Pigeon Forge Parkway on my way to work."

Rydetha shook her head in disbelief, but it had nothing to do with Ian's death. Her focus was on Camille's hands. "Girl, hand me those jeans. You'll never get your clothes in that bag if you don't roll them tighter than that."

"Fine. I've tried rolling them three times. I can't do it as tight as you can."

Rydetha glanced at the two bags sitting on the floor beside the bed. "I thought you were taking three bags?"

"I am, but the T bag is packed already."

"A tea bag?"

"T as in travel. It fits behind the seat on the sissy bar. I'll use it as a backrest. I hope I haven't forgotten anything. She pulled a slip of paper from her jeans pocket . . . phone, check; jacket, check; zip in liner; poncho, flashlight, first aid kit, toiletries, clothes, check. I think that's it. Now to strap on the tent, the way Ian showed me."

"Tent?"

"Yep. It's a seven-hour ride, riding straight through. I'll probably set up camp about half-way."

"Heavenly days! Please tell me you aren't staying in a tent . . . alone."

Camille shrugged. "Fine. If it'll make you feel better, I'll ask someone to join me."

"Don't be facetious." She plunked her hands on her hips. "I declare, Camille Benrey, this gets crazier by the minute."

"So you've said." She glanced at her watch. "I think I'm ready. Can you think of anything I might have forgotten?"

"Besides common sense?" Her eyes expressed her fears. "Please be careful, hon. Don't talk to strangers. I don't trust those weird looking bikers with all those evil-looking tattoos. You stay away from them, you hear?"

Camille grinned. "Yes, *Mother.*"

Rydetha plunked her hands on her hips. "I may not be your mother, but someone needs to try to talk sense into you."

"You're profiling, Deedee.

"Profiling, my foot. I'm telling you what everyone but you seems to know."

"But it's not true. There are bad apples in every walk of life, but Ian assured me there are no finer people anywhere, than bikers. He said, 'They'll have your back, Cami, when I'm not there to take care of you.'"

"And I suppose he said it all in the middle of the night, after he died. Am I right?" She groaned as if she couldn't believe the hurtful words were spewing from her own mouth.

CHAPTER 9

Camille sensed Deedee's immediate regret for being sarcastic, but there was no need for her to hide her feelings. It wasn't as if her pretense fooled Camille for even a minute into believing she'd had a sudden change of heart.

"Deedee, I know you don't believe me, but I haven't made any of it up. I admit it sounds impossible, but if I remember correctly, you're the one who told me more than once that there's nothing impossible with God."

Deedee nodded. "True, but . . ." Her voice trailed off.

"But? There's a *but*? You're saying nothing is impossible with God, but?" Her chin quivered. "Ian's visits have turned my life around, Deedee. For a long time, I've had no desire to live. I had no desire to play. The love of my life—the one who made me laugh, play and enjoy life was gone. I went through the motions of going to school to become a nurse, but I'd lost all interest in helping others, when I didn't know how to help myself. I'd reached the lowest level. And then, Ian came one night and put me back on the right track. My interest in school, in living, playing and loving was renewed. The whole world changed from gray to an array of vivid colors. Life became beautiful again. Can that be so wrong?"

Deedee's pinched face suddenly lit up. She threw her arms in the air. "Well, glory! No, sweetheart. That can't be wrong. That's great news to my ears."

Camille eyed her with suspicion. To think Deedee had suddenly experienced an epiphany appeared a bit suspect.

"I won't deny that ever since you've had . . . uh . . . these strange manifestations, your attitude toward life has changed for the better. It's been good seeing you laugh again. But a few minutes ago, I thought you'd resigned yourself to live the lonely, miserable existence of a brokenhearted widow when you expressed no desire to ever marry. I'm glad you're at least open to loving again. That's a start."

"Deedee, when I said my interest in living, playing and loving was renewed, I was saying I'm living *again,* playing *again*, and loving *still.* I never stopped loving. I loved Ian when he was with me and I don't love him one bit less now that he's gone. I'll always love him. He knows that."

"Okay, I'll hush, but I won't stop hoping. Send me your address when you get settled, and I'll ship your things to you."

"Don't bother. Keep anything you want and take the rest to the Christian Mission. I'll buy whatever basics I need after I get to Mobile. Did I ever tell you my grandparents lived in Mobile when I was little?"

"You mentioned it. I suppose you'll look them up?"

"No, they both died years ago, but I never knew them. Seems they had a falling out with my Mom before I was born. Mom never talked about her parents, but I searched for them on the Internet after I left home and found them both listed in the obits."

"I'm sorry, sweetie."

She shrugged. "No big deal. I have one set of grandparents and I'm not sure I could handle another set if they're all alike."

"Cami, I don't mean to meddle, but don't you think it's time to forgive your Mom and Dad for whatever it is you're holding against them?"

"No way. You don't understand. Mom not only lied to me, but she lied to . . . to the man she said was my father. Jacob Gorham is a cold, hard man, but I now understand. She made him that way. I can't imagine the pain he lives with daily, knowing she tricked him into marrying him when she was pregnant with me."

Her jaw dropped. "You aren't serious."

"I'm dead serious."

She shuddered. "I wish you wouldn't use that term. . . especially at a time such as this. So your Mom actually told you she was pregnant with you and tricked a man into marrying her?"

"No. He told me."

"You mean your father?"

"My father? I have no clue who that would be."

"So were you close to . . . to the man who raised you?"

"That would be the butler, but I'm sure you mean Jacob Gorham. The truth is, he was closer to Tope than he was to me. That's what he called Topaz, his Golden Retriever. He loved that dog, but his money and his dog were the only two things that ever mattered to him. The day I left home, I learned the truth. He was drunk so I felt it was my lucky break. It was always easier to get what I wanted if he was drunk, rather than to wait for him to sober up. I'd recently found a nice condo near the university I wanted, so I asked for a check for the down payment." Her voice cracked. "I'll never forget how he glared at me. It scared me when he staggered over and ran his fingers through my hair. I thought he was gonna pull it, but he turned loose and said, 'It was red when you were born.'"

Rydetha grinned. "Red? Your hair? He really *was* drunk, wasn't he?"

"Actually, it's true and I've seen pictures to prove it. I was a little carrot-top when I was born. It didn't begin to change until I started kindergarten. I wish it had stayed that color."

"What do you think he was getting at?"

"I figure one of Mom's boyfriends was a redhead, and Dad . . . uh, Jacob . . . figured it out, since neither he nor Mom have red hair. That's when he went crazy and spilled the beans. He said I was over eighteen and he was through supporting another man's

76

kid. I felt as if someone stabbed me in the gut when he yelled, 'You want money? Go ask your Daddy.' It made me sick on my stomach to think how Mom preached to me about 'saving myself,' as she called it, then to learn two men had reason to believe they were responsible for getting her pregnant disgusted me. Heaven knows how many more men there were."

"Camille, people change. Maybe the reason she preached to you was to protect you from making the same mistakes. It's been years since she heard from you. Please call her before you strike out on this trip."

A wry smile crept across her face. "Before I strike out? You still don't think I'll live to see the other side of Deals Gap, do you?"

"I didn't say that, but you know it's a possibility. You've never been on a trip alone, and to start out on such a dangerous trek is insane."

"Face it, Deedee. You're terrified of motorcycles. I understand. I was like you the day I was thumbing and Ian stopped to pick me up. If I hadn't been so anxious to get out of town, I wouldn't have considered crawling on the back of a motorcycle, but once we were on the road, it was the most exhilarating feeling. It gave me a completely different perspective."

"Weren't you scared? Of him, I mean? I can't imagine what you were thinking to get on a bike with a stranger, who could've been a serial killer. The hilarious part is that you were probably one of the few people who wouldn't have known Ian Benrey."

Rydetha followed her out the door and watched Camille strap a tent to the shiny pink and black motorcycle.

Camille said, "I know you can't understand, but I've felt so much closer to Ian as I packed for this trip. It seemed as if he was telling me what to carry. Things I'd forgotten, are coming back. For instance, I'd finished packing, and it wasn't verbal, but I heard his voice in my head, saying, 'Don't forget to wrap your bags in plastic in case it rains. The bags may leak.'"

"Oh, Camille, You wanna talk omens? This sounds like an omen to me. You say you feel closer to Ian now, and I fear you're closer than you realize. Don't you see what's happening here? You're still going through the grief process and aren't thinking straight."

"You're wrong, Rydetha. My head is clearer than it's been since Ian died."

"Well, it's ridiculous to make your first long trip alone, but it's utterly insane to consider taking on Deals Gap. It's not as if you can't bypass it. Please, please, reconsider."

"You're sweet, but you're a worry-wart."

"And for good reason. Have you never heard of the Tree of Shame, where all the seasoned bikers who thought they were savvy enough to make the Tail of the Dragon, discovered they weren't as savvy as they thought? Nothing is left of their fancy motorcycles but a metal heap. You think you know more than they did?"

She shrugged. "Face it, Rydetha. Neither of us are gonna change our mind. I'll miss you." She hugged her tightly, then reached up and blotted a tear from Rydetha's face. "Please, don't worry. I'll be fine. Honest." She crawled up on the bike and gripped the handlebars. "Mobile, here I come."

"You know you're breaking my heart. Don't forget to call."

"I won't. Pray for me?"

"Every minute until I know you're safe in Mobile. How long will it be before the settlement from Ian's accident comes in?"

"Please don't call it an accident. The man didn't accidentally get drunk. He'd had four previous collisions caused from being intoxicated. It was no accident that he was driving without a license. The night he ran into Ian and left the scene, he didn't even have his lights on. As for the insurance, I think they're still wrangling, but I have no desire to profit from Ian's death."

"Do you have enough money to live on until then?"

"I will have, if I get this job."

"And what if you don't?"

"Rydetha, if there's one thing I've learned since Ian's death, it's to take one day at the time, for none of us know what tomorrow will bring. I know he'd be so proud of me for finishing school. If I land this job at Trinity Hospital, it'll be a dream come true."

"And if the interview doesn't work out or the job isn't what you imagined, will you be coming back here?"

"One day at the time, Rydetha. One day at the time. I'll think about tomorrow when tomorrow comes."

She pursed her lips. "Haven't you heard? Tomorrow never

comes."

"Then I have nothing to worry about, do I?" A lump too big to swallow caused her to choke, as she glared at the half-heart, which Ian painted on the back of both their helmets, the day they married at the Wedding Chapel. *You'll always be the other half of my heart, Ian Benrey.* She buckled it under her chin and waved goodbye to her teary-eyed spectator.

Rydetha lifted her hand in a reluctant wave. "God speed, my precious friend," she whispered, watching Camille ride off in the early morning hours, just as the sun peeked over the horizon. "I earnestly pray you prove me wrong, sweet girl."

CHAPTER 10

Camille checked the weather on her phone and couldn't have wished for a better day to make the seven-and-a-half-hour trip. The wind was to her back and with the sun hid behind the gently rolling clouds, the first leg of the trip was quite enjoyable. She could almost feel Ian riding beside her, praising her for being so brave.

All was well until she spotted a huge sign bearing the likeness of a dragon with a long tail, causing her first wave of panic. As she rounded a sharp curve, a Mazda Miata convertible zoomed around her as if she were standing still. Before she could catch her breath, four bikers flew by. She gauged her speed with the next group of bikers, staying with them all the way, although the speed felt much faster on curves than when driving in her neighborhood. She spotted a dark blue Harley like Ian's and pretended it was him, which boosted her confidence.

Without warning, the low-lying clouds burst open, dumping heavy, hammering rain. The term "gully-washer" flashed through her mind. How much deeper could they get? She glanced down on either side at the drop-off and tightened her grip on the handlebars while questioning her sanity. Not that she was afraid to die, but she wasn't fond of pain. *What if?* She swallowed hard.. She looked ahead, then behind. She'd been so consumed with fear, she apparently had slowed down and failed to notice she was once again traveling alone.

The darkened sky gave little evidence of the pounding rain letting up any time soon. Then, spotting a dive with a host of motorcycles parked out front, Cami swerved into the parking lot. The inside was quaint with its hewn timber walls and crude-built booths. A waitress lumbered over, and without making eye contact, mumbled, "Whatcha want?"

"Hamburger and Lemonade."

"We ain't got no lemonade. Got lemons and water. Make your own."

She spotted sugar on the table. "Fine. I'll take water with lemon." No one paid attention until she pulled off her helmet and shook her long hair loose. Seeing heads turn her way, she almost turned around to get back on the road.

Four scary-looking brutes sat in a booth across from her. A big guy with beady eyes and an unkempt beard said, "Hey, miss. Where ya' headed?"

Her throat tightened. Suddenly, leather, beards and durags that had never made her nervous when she was with Ian, now caused her heart to thump erratically. She took a sip of lemonade. "Uh, south. Going south."

"Anywhere in particular?"

"Uh . . . No," her voice cracked as she suspiciously eyed each head turned in her direction. "I mean, yes. Gulf Coast. Uh . . . Mobile. . . In particular." She grimaced.

He slid off the bench and walked over to the booth where she sat. A sneak peek out of the corner of her eye revealed a giant of a man. Cami took a bite of the hamburger, hoping to stop the teeth chattering. *Please, please, don't sit down.*

With a slight gesture of his head, he motioned toward his buddies. "We're on our way to a little place called Pascagoula. Ever hear of it?"

"No."

"It's in Mississippi." He held out a hand that was broad enough to wrap around her neck. The thought made her shudder. She slowly extended her arm and grasped the rough, calloused hand.

"The name's Clyde. Better known as Cross-Tee." Three big men rose from where they sat, strutted over and stood looking down, making her even more nervous than the curves. An older guy with a long white beard said, "You're welcome to ride with us, Not good for you to ride alone. Have you ever done the Tail before?"

"No."

Cross-Tee said, "Ma'am, I'm getting the feeling we frighten you. I gather you haven't been riding long?"

So, it was that evident. The men were courteous and appeared harmless enough, but how could she be sure? She tried to picture Cross-Tee playing jolly ol' Santa at the mall, which helped somewhat.

The other three—introduced as Frog, Oz and Catfish--reached out for handshakes.

She gave a slight nod. "Camille. Camille Benrey."

They glanced at one another and smiled. "Benrey. Of course. Chap's wife."

"No, I'm afraid you have me confused with someone else. My husband's name was Ian." She cringed, wishing she hadn't used the past tense. Perhaps it would've been safer for them to think her husband was still alive.

"Yes ma'am. Ian was a good friend of ours. We knew him well. He was Chap to us. Short for Chaplain. So are you riding the bike Ian ordered for your Christmas present?"

"You knew about the bike?"

"I reckon we did! It's all Chap could talk about for weeks. My condolences. I know you miss him. We miss him, too. I seem to recall he referred to you as Cami?"

"He did!" The erratic thumping in her chest slowed to a steady beat. " I'd like it if you'd call me Cami, also." Ian's friends. How cool was that? Surely God had arranged this trip. If it hadn't been for that sudden downpour, she would never have met this great group of men. She recalled Ian saying, "Bikers are your friends. They'll have your back when I'm not there." Did he have a premonition his time on earth was coming to an end? She'd heard people say things to that effect, though she'd never believed it. Not until now.

The rain stopped. Cross-Tee turned to his buddies. "Anyone interested in seeing what's happening in Mobile, before going on to Pascagoula?"

One by one, hands raised as each one said, "I'm in."

Cami glanced from one gentle face to another and wondered what it was about these four kind-hearted souls that had frightened her. She reached out for hugs. "It's great to meet Ian's friends, and I'm honored to have the opportunity to ride with you guys. Thank you."

"Awesome, Li'l Darlin'."

She giggled. "Li'l Darlin'?"

"Suits you. Do you mind?"

"Sweet! Don't mind at all." If only Ian could see her now.

"We'll stop about every hour or so to give you a chance to stretch your legs."

"Oh don't do any favors for me. I'll be fine."

"Stopping is good, and unless you're in a hurry to get there, even with the stops, we can have you there by nightfall."

"Then let's ride, guys. We've got a lot of road to cover."

CHAPTER 11

The sun had begun to set over Mobile Bay, as Cami and her newfound friends rode across the Parkway. Never had she seen a more beautiful sight as the brilliant orange rays reflected over the sparkling waters.

They stopped at an Oyster Bar, although the thought of slicky, slimy creatures sliding down her throat made her shudder. She ordered fried shrimp and watched in horror as the guys guzzled down dozens of raw oysters, drenched in hot sauce.

Cross-Tee suggested they save room for dessert and stop at a Mobile diner called "Bubba's," which met with no objections. Cami couldn't imagine how any of the guys could possibly eat dessert, after the number of oysters they consumed.

The diner didn't look like much from the outside. but stepping inside, she was stunned to see the place packed. A big redheaded fellow who made Cross-Tee look like his little brother, gave out a loud, friendly whoop when he spotted them walking through the door.

"Well, I be June bug, if it ain't the Big Tee. Where ya' been keeping yourself, bud? What's it been? Two years? Three?"

Cross-Tee rushed over with open arms and embraced the man they called Bubba. "More like four. I've been trying to find a reason to get down this way, and I finally found one." He motioned for Cami.

"Bubba, d'ya remember Ian Benrey?"

"Of course, I do. I sure hated to hear of his accident. There'll never be another Ian."

"Well, this li'l darlin' is his wife, Cami."

Cami thrust out her hand, expecting a handshake, but instead the big guy leaned down and wrapped her in his arms. "God Bless you, shug. My sincere condolences. Your husband . . . he was . . ." He stopped and pressed his lips together. This huge bearded man appeared to choke back tears. "Ian was a good, Godly man—one of the best, but I'm sure I'm not telling you something you don't already know."

"Yes, he was. Thank you."

Bubba said, "Ya'll have a seat and my waitress will take your order shortly. She's entertaining the church group at the moment, so I may have to pull her away. The College and Career Class from the church down the street drop by after services every Wednesday evening for dessert." His lip curled upward. "My cute little waitress is sweet on one of my customers."

Bubba walked over to the table and tapped a handsome young man on the back of the head. "Jamal, stop flirting with my help. She has customers."

The waitress giggled and ran over with a pad and pencil in her hand. "Hi, sorry to keep you waiting. Didn't see you come in."

Bubba said, "She doesn't see anything or anyone when that ugly brute, Jamal, walks in here. I may have to fire her."

Her nose crinkled. "Don't mind that bag o' wind. He couldn't do without me and he knows it. I'm Lexie, and I'll be taking care of you. The dinner hour is over, but we have sandwiches and pie." She handed out menus. You'll find them listed on the back."

Bubba shook his head. "It's not over for these guys. Whatever you want, fellows. Name it and I'll be happy to fix it."

Cross Tee said, "We stopped for oysters on the Bay, Bubba. Naturally, we wanted to see you, but mainly we came to get one of your famous coconut pies. You do still make them, don't you?"

"The sun still rises in the East, doesn't it? I have two left, and you guys need to finish them off."

The waitress brought the pies and five plates to the table. Cami shook her head and pushed her plate aside. "No thanks. It looks delicious, but I couldn't eat a thing."

Bubba sat down at their table and the men caught up on the past, reliving funny stories. Boisterous laughter filled the room.

The waitress motioned for Cami. "Psst, it's awfully loud over there. Would you like to join me at the table in the corner?"

Cami smiled. "But don't you need to take care of the

customers in the back room?"

She shrugged. "They're regulars. They take care of themselves. Are you from Mobile?"

"No. I'm from . . ." She swallowed hard. "From Sevierville, Tennessee."

"Then welcome to Mobile. My name's Lexie."

"Hi, Lexie. I'm Cami Benrey."

"You just passing through?"

"I sure hope not. I have an interview in the morning at ten o'clock at the Hospital on Airport. I'm praying I get the job."

"Cool. Follow me."

"But where . . . "

Lexie strolled over to the long table in the back room. "Guys, I have someone I'd like you to meet. This is Cami Benrey from Sevierville, Tennessee, and she has an interview in Mobile tomorrow. She needs us to pray that if this is where God would have her to be, that she'll get the job."

A girl said, "Benrey? And you're from Sevierville? I don't suppose you were related to Ian Benrey."

Cami lowered her head. "Ian was my husband." She swallowed hard, hearing the low groans around the table.

"Husband? Oh, I'm so sorry. He had such a beautiful voice."

Cami considered it ironic that so many people knew and loved her husband, yet she had never heard of him until after she'd fallen in love with him. She thought back to the day she was thumbing a ride and wondered if that wasn't the very day she fell in love. Of course, it was. She loved him from the first moment she laid eyes on him . . . although she didn't recognize it was love until the night she accidentally crossed the Red Sea.

Cami listened as the guy they called Jamal led in one of the sweetest prayers she'd ever heard. All her anxieties melted and she could hardly wait to get to the motel to call Deedee. But perhaps Deedee already knew. Was it a coincidence she met Ian's best friends while traveling Deal's Gap? Or yet another coincidence that she wound up in a little diner off the beaten path where there just happened to be a group of Christians who chose to pray for her? Not likely. No, she was quite confident the events of this day were coordinated by God in response to Rydetha Morgan's prayers.

The church group cleared out and Cross-Tee said, "Bubba, it was great seeing you again. I'm thrilled to hear you're getting married. Super!"

"Thanks, Tee. I hope you and the guys can make it."

"Wouldn't miss it. We're heading to Pascagoula, but we'll be back in time to see you tie the knot." He said, "Li'l Darlin', if you're ready to get back on the road, we'll ride you to your motel and see that you get there safely."

Lexie said, "Where are you staying?"

"I have reservations at a motel on Airport Boulevard, near the Hospital. If I get the job, I'll be looking for an apartment to rent."

"I don't suppose you'd want a roommate, would you?"

"You?"

"Yeah. I'm renting a room in a small cottage with Bubba's fiancé, but after the wedding, Bubba will be moving in. They've assured me they have no plans to kick me out, but it's much too tiny for newlyweds and one more. My problem is trying to find a decent apartment in a good neighborhood that I can afford on my salary."

Cami threw up her hand for a high-five. "Girl, you just found yourself a roommate."

"Awesome. Call me after your interview and I'll give you a list of places to go look. I have to work tomorrow and won't get off until late, or I'd go with you."

Bubba overheard the conversation. "I'll call Keely and get her to fill in for you, Lexie. Trey's out of town and she'll probably want to hang out here, anyway."

"Thanks, Bubba. That's great."

Cami said, "In that case, I'll ride over after the interview tomorrow and pick you up, Lexie. That is . . . if I get the job."

"You'll get it. I know you will. See you tomorrow." Lexie followed them out the door. Her eyes widened when she saw Cami strapping on a helmet. "That bike . . . that's *yours?*"

Cami smiled. "Oh, I didn't think to tell you. Are you afraid to ride?"

"Afraid? Are you kidding? I wish I could afford one. Oh, this is gonna be fun. A biker roomie. Awesome!

After escorting her to her motel, the four good Samaritans waved goodbye, and for a split second, Camille thought she saw her husband ride off with them. Funny the tricks the mind can play when one wants something so badly that insanity takes over. She shivered. At least, that's how Deedee would've attempted to explain.

****

Cami could see the hospital from the motel. Her twelfth-floor suite surpassed her expectations, but tonight she was so tired she could've slept outside. Tears welled in her eyes, remembering a stormy night when she slept in a tent—the night Ian accused her of crossing the Red Sea. It seemed so very long ago. After dressing for bed, she switched out the light, set the alarm, pulled back the duvet cover and slid between cool, crisp sheets. The bed felt so wide . . . so empty. *Why, God? Why my Ian?*

It must've been shortly after midnight when she felt a hand rubbing against her cheek. "Ian?" She whispered. "Oh, Ian, I've missed you so. How did you find me?"

"You didn't really think you could hide from me, did you babe?" His strong arms wrapped around her, pulling her close.

She buried her face in his chest and whispered, "I did it, Ian. I did it for you."

"Did what, sweetheart?"

"Rode the Tail of the Dragon."

"I know."

"You do?"

"Of course. I was right behind you, making sure you got to

92

Mobile safely."

"Really? I didn't see you."

"Cami, God has used various means to speak to his people through the ages. Just because the eye doesn't see a dream, a vision or an angel, doesn't make it any less real."

"Are you saying . . . ?"

"Yes."

She batted her eyes and tried hard to see his image in the darkened room, but it was too dark. But Ian, I saw you when . . . "

"When did you see me, Cami?" "

Was he purposely trying to confuse her? Her mind raced. "Remember the night I walked down to the basement with you?"

"What was I wearing?"

"Wearing? It was dark. But I saw you, Ian. I did. I was amazed that you had no scars from the accident."

"Did you turn on a light when you walked downstairs?"

Her heart raced. So Rydetha was right. There was no light. But how—"

"You saw me, babe, but not with your eyes. You saw with your heart. Don't forget to always live right, play hard and love long."

"Oh, Ian. Don't go. Please don't go." She reached over and switched on the light, but he was gone.

CHAPTER 12

Thursday morning, Camille awoke and tried to remember exactly what happened after she fell asleep last night. Could Deedie have been right? A dream? She rubbed her face, then gazed in the mirror. No. It was *not* dream. Her pink cheek was chafed from her precious husband's five-o'clock shadow rubbing against her tender skin.

She laid out her black dress and felt a shiver. Maybe it was superstitious and crazy, but the word "omen," kept invading her thoughts and this was no time for negative vibes, regardless of how silly they might be. She quickly undressed and pulled out the crisp green and white floral, then nodded her endorsement at the professional-looking image in the mirror. *Nice!* Deedee would approve, especially since she was the one who packed it.

Cami glanced at her watch as she paced the floor in her motel room. Eight-forty-five. One hour and fifteen minutes before time for the interview. Seventy-five long minutes to imagine all sorts of terrifying scenarios. If only time would pass so she could stop dreading it.

She pulled her hair up in a ponytail, then placed the brush in her bag and tied a durag around her head.

Deedee had asked what she'd do if she didn't get the job. Until now, it hadn't been a serious concern, since she was confident the position was hers. Why wouldn't she get it? She finished first in her class and had a great recommendation from the head nurse, where she worked while in school.

Apple Annie. Deedee's words rang in Cami's ears. If two applicants showed up for the interview and one looked like Apple Annie, which one . . . she swallowed hard. Though she'd never seen the movie, she was quite confident Apple Annie would not be a famous cardiologist's first choice.

She jerked off the durag and brushed out her long wavy locks. Why take the chance? It was only a few blocks to the hospital and a beautiful day for a walk. She took one last glance in the mirror, swallowed her fear, then headed down Airport Boulevard to the Hospital.

****

Cami arrived twenty minutes early and was immediately escorted by the receptionist into a beautiful office overlooking a man-made lake.

Dr. Cunningham stood and extended his hand. His warm smile

put her at ease. After a few minutes of small talk, he said "Camille, if you should need help finding a place to stay, I have a daughter-in-law about your age and I'm sure she'd be happy to show you around and help you get settled."

"You mean . . . are you saying I have the job?"

"Absolutely. This interview was a formality. Dr. Odom and Dr. Harris assured me you're the best, and their recommendations were all I needed. You had the job before you walked in. And I must say, you're even prettier than your picture. Would you like for me to call my daughter-in-law and have her help you find an apartment?"

"That's very kind, Dr. Cunningham, but I met someone last night at a little diner, and she's also looking for a place, so we plan to room together."

"I see."

"From the expression on your face, I'm not sure you do. What's wrong?"

"Maybe nothing." He leaned back in his chair and crossed his arms over his chest. "Okay, I'm going to put on my 'daddy cap.'"

"I'm not following you."

"I'm going to talk to you as I would if you were my daughter—and not as someone in my employ. Do you mind?"

"Not at all. I'm just not sure what I said that seems to have you so concerned." Cami waited for his response.

"I think you should think twice before agreeing to sign a contract for an apartment with a stranger you happened to meet at a diner. It's a shame we can no longer take a person at their word and trust them to be honest and sincere, but these are perilous times we live in. I hope you'll reconsider."

"I do appreciate your concern, and I understand. Maybe it sounds crazy, but I consider myself to be a pretty good judge of character, and I have good vibes about this girl. We connected immediately."

"Good vibes? Camille, I understand from everyone I've talked to about you, that you're a very compassionate young woman. That's definitely a quality I look for in my nurses. However, a drawback sometimes comes with that wonderful attribute."

"And that *is*—?"

"Being *too* trusting. Why rush it? There's a very nice motel with extended stay suites in walking distance to the hospital. It would be a great place to stay until you find what you're searching for. Your salary should allow you to find a decent place, without having to have a roommate. In a few months, you'll have had time to make plenty of friends, and if the idea of sharing an apartment still appeals to you, you can be selective."

"Thank you, doctor. Although I honestly don't feel your concern is warranted in this case, I hear what you're saying, and I appreciate the advice. But I promised Lexie I'd pick her up at the diner after the interview. I'd feel like a heel if I went back on my word. I trust her, and I'd feel ashamed if I should give her a reason not to trust me."

The lines on his forehead went away as a smile inched across his lips. "Did you say Lexie?"

"Yes. She's a waitress at the diner."

"Well, that's different. Why didn't you say you were talking about Lex? You had me worried, but you two will get along great. She's a sweetheart—but why is Lexie looking for another place to stay? She has a room at—" He popped his palm to his forehead. "Of course! She needs to relocate because Bubba will be moving into his fiancé's house after they're married."

"Then you know her, and you approve?"

"I not only approve, I think it's a perfect fit for you both. My daughter-in-law, Keely, and Lexie are best friends."

"Keely is your daughter-in-law?"

"Married to my only son. So, you two have met?"

"Not yet, but Bubba said he'd call Keely to work in Lexie's place today while we go apartment hunting. I believe he said Keely is his niece?"

"Correct. My son works out-of-town a lot and Keely often helps Bubba at the diner when Trey's off on assignment." He stood and reached out his hand. "I'm needed in OR this morning, so what if you come in tomorrow, say around lunch. We'll go over a few details, and then you can officially start on the first of the month. That gives you and Lexie a few days to find a place."

Cami made a real effort to remain poised, when her instinct prodded her to jump up and down, squealing. Deedie would be so relieved when she called to tell her how perfectly things were working out for her. She reached out her hand. "See you tomorrow.

Thank you, Dr. Cunningham."

"Fine. Sorry I don't have more time this morning. Say about twelvish, tomorrow?"

"I'll be here."

"I'll walk you down the hall and have one of the nurses show you around the hospital. I'm looking forward to having you as my head nurse." His smile faded. "Uh . . . one more thing, Camille. I don't know how to say this, without sounding . . ." He chewed on his lower lip. "It's actually embarrassing that I'd need to bring it up. The thing is . . . I probably should warn you . . ." He stopped, then shrugged it off. "Forget it. If it becomes a problem, we'll deal with it."

Warn me? Her muscles tightened. Things had gone too smoothly. She should've known it was too good to be true. Why was he hesitating? Her trust in the man was slowly eroding.

CHAPTER 13

Willa, a sweet-looking gray-haired nurse with a big smile, met Cami outside Dr. Cunningham's office door.

"Welcome to Trinity Hospital, Camille. We'll start the tour by introducing you to the other nurses."

"Thank you, Willa, but please, . . . call me Cami."

"Then Cami, it is."

They stopped at the Nurses Desk and Willa introduced her to Dianne, an attractive brunette in her early forties.

Dianne eyed her suspiciously, then said, "So you're Camille, the chosen one?"

"Chosen one?" Cami swallowed hard. "I'm not sure I understand." Truth was, she didn't understand at all. The sly remark had a threatening sound to it.

Dianne smirked. "Nothing to explain. Carlos . . . oops!" She popped her hand over her mouth. Then glancing down the hall, she said, "Uh, Dr. Cunningham had more than enough applicants to choose from on his staff, but he chose you." She eyed her from head to foot. "Of course, it's not hard to figure out. You're young. Probably just finished school, am I right?"

"Excuse me? I'm not following you."

Dianne glanced at a nurse nearby and winked. "No? Well, maybe you aren't as smart as you look. I assumed you'd understand what it means to finish school." She snickered. "But then, perhaps you didn't finish? Not to worry. I have a feeling you have all the credentials you need for the job you were hired to do."

A hefty nurse with bleached blonde hair covered her mouth. "Watch it, Dianne. You're gonna say too much and get us in trouble." Dianne shook her head, then whispered to her co-conspirator in a low, coarse voice. Cami had a gut feeling the words were meant to be heard.

"She's fresh out of school, Carla, so I suppose the doctor expects us to coddle her since she lacks experience."

Carla pursed her lips. "Oh, I imagine she's had plenty of experience."

Willa's face turned red. "Stop it. We heard every word you said, which I'm sure was your intent. If you could see the impressive resume, you'd understand why Dr. Cunningham picked her over either of you."

Cami said, "Thanks, Willa, but I hope to prove I need no defense. I'm confident I can handle the duties required of my job."

Dianne grinned. "Well, you're in luck. The duties that Carlos . . . uh, Dr. Cunningham requires won't involve baths or bed pans. At least, not for *patients*." Her remark drew snickers from Carla.

Cami seethed. If this hip-swinging, foul-talking forty-something female thought she'd run her off with her sharp tongue, she had another think coming. Cami could only assume the resentment stemmed from the likelihood that either Carla or Dianne—or both—had applied for the position. Dianne appeared to have slipped twice and called Dr. Cunningham by his first name. Perhaps she not only was familiar with him on a professional level, but a personal level as well. Did that account for the hostility? Could it be she was having an affair with the man?

Cami guessed the doctor to be in his early fifties, but there was no denying he was ruggedly handsome. Tall and muscular, dark hair with a hint of gray at the temples—he had the striking good-looks of a model. Understandable that he'd have brazen nurses vying for his after-hours attention and Cami was confident she'd just become acquainted with two prime contenders. They could rest easy. She had no interest in competing. Although she'd been taken aback by the doctor's looks at first glance, she also thought a Lamborghini was a handsome automobile—yet, she'd never entertained the thought of parking one in *her* garage. Dr. Cunningham had acted very professional and had given her no reason to see him as anything but a highly-respected, physician. Her pulse raced. But wouldn't the nurses who had worked with him for years, know him better than she did?

Now, his last words bothered her even more. She mulled them over in her head. *"It's actually embarrassing that I'd need to bring it up, Cami. The thing is . . . I probably should warn you . . ."* Chills ran down her spine. He ended with, *"Forget it. If it becomes a problem, we'll deal with it."*

Why didn't he say what he meant? Cami could hardly breathe, when she recalled what appeared at the time to be nothing more than a casual compliment, when he remarked, "You're even prettier than your picture." It sounded quite innocent, but now the pieces were falling into place. If Dr. Cunningham had the notion she might want to join his harem, he was grossly mistaken.

She dared not mention the incident to Lexie, being she was best friends with the doctor's daughter-in-law. Cami couldn't afford to quit. She *wouldn't* quit. She needed this job and now that she'd been put on alert, she knew what signs to look for. She'd let Romeo know from the get-go that she had no desire to become a new notch on his belt. If, after that, she still had a job, she'd handle problems as they arose.

CHAPTER 14

The remainder of the Hospital tour was quite pleasant—but the gnawing question lurked in the back of Cami's mind. How many of the personnel secretly felt she was not hired on her merits, but chosen for her looks?

At the end of the tour, Cami walked back to the motel and called Lexie. "Hey, Lex . . . I got the job."

Lexie squealed in the phone. "Awesome. I'm thrilled for you, Cami. And for *me*, also, of course, since I now have a roomie." There was a pause, then Lexie said, "Is something wrong?"

"Why do you ask?"

"I don't know. I guess I expected you to be more excited. Aren't you happy?"

"Happy? Of course. Why wouldn't I be? It's the perfect job."

"Great. I'm sure you're exhausted from the stress."

"Yeah, but the stressful part is over." She could only hope it was true. "I'll pick you up at the diner after I change."

"I'll be ready. I found four places to check out, but if we don't find something we like, I have an option to run by you."

"I'm listening."

"My grandparents eat breakfast at the diner every morning, and when they realized I'd have to move, they offered to let us stay in the garage apartment back of their house. When Bubba was growing up, his family lived there. His mother worked as a maid and his daddy was the gardener. His parents died years ago, and he's been living in a small bungalow near the diner for ages. The garage apartment has been vacant for years, but Paw-Paw said we could stay rent free if we were willing to paint it and put in new appliances. He says the old stove and refrigerator need replacing, but other than that, there's nothing major. I'll understand if you'd rather live in a condo or more modern apartment, but I wanted to throw out the option."

"Rent free? That sounds a little scary. I've always heard if something sounds too good to be true, it probably is. What's the neighborhood like? I'd want to feel safe if we lived there, since I could be coming home at midnight some nights."

"True, it's an older neighborhood, but a very exclusive area. The houses are gorgeous, and it's in a gated community. Paw-Paw was a banker before he retired, and they've lived there forty years."

"I don't get it. If the apartment belongs to your grandparents, why haven't you been living there?"

"Long story, but the short of it is, I didn't know they were my grandparents until months after I was settled in. By then, I was happy where I was, so the subject of moving never came up. I've visited Maw-Maw and Paw-Paw many times but never had a reason to go inside the apartment."

"We'll definitely check it out. I'll pick you up in about fifteen minutes."

"Perfect. Keely isn't here yet, but she should be here by the time you arrive."

Cami rode over to the diner and Bubba opened the door and threw up his hand for a high-five. "Congratulations. I hear you got the job."

"Thank you." She glanced around the dining room. "Keely's not here, is she? If you need Lexie, we can do this later."

"Are you kidding? You may can wait, but I'm not sure Lexie can. Truthfully, I think she's more excited about riding on the back of the bike than she is in finding a place to live. I hope the two of you find exactly what you're looking for."

"Thanks, Bubba, and congratulations on your upcoming marriage. Lexie's told me all about your beautiful fiancé, and she sounds like a very special lady. Frankly, I'm thrilled you're getting married."

"Why is that?"

"If not for the wedding, I wouldn't be getting a roommate."

His body shook when he laughed. "Happy to oblige. To be honest, Cami, I still pinch myself and wonder if this sweet, precious jewel is really gonna marry a worn-out ol' geezer like me."

"Hey, from what I hear, your Jewel is getting a real prize."

"Thanks. Allow me to give you a personal invitation to the wedding. The wedding is Keely's doings." He cocked his head back and laughed. "She'll be here shortly. You haven't met Keely, have you?

"No, but I look forward to meeting both Keely and your Jewel."

His eyes squinted. "Keely and who?" Without waiting for an answer, he snapped his fingers. "Oh . . . my jewel!"

Cami nodded.

"The Keeper and the Jewel. That's my girls. If it was left up to me we would've gone to the Court House and tied the knot." He let out a long sigh. "But Keely insists it would be selfish to deny our friends the joy of helping to celebrate." He grinned, while shaking his head, dismissively. "So, a wedding is going down. Arguing with that niece of mine is like arguing with a fence post. Well, I didn't mean to keep you. You and Lexie enjoy your afternoon and take all the time you need. I hear you're considering the little apartment where I grew up."

Lexie shrugged. "I'm thinking Cami and I should look at the other four possibilities before checking out the garage apartment."

Bubba's brow lifted. "Really? Why is that?"

She giggled. "Because I'm afraid if we go to Maw-Maw and Paw-Paw's first, it will be our last stop and I want to spend more time riding around West Mobile on the back of the bike."

Cami smiled. "Oh, trust me, we'll have plenty of time for that later."

The door to the diner opened and a perky young woman rushed in and addressed Cami. "Hi. I'm Keely, and there's no mistaking who you are. I've heard so much about you. It's a pleasure to finally meet you. I had dinner with my husband's parents last night, and you were the topic of conversation. Dad said he'd finally found what he'd been looking for."

Cami squirmed. "Dr. Cunningham seems nice."

"Nice? He's the best." She bit her lip. "Well, I suppose it's a tie, since his son is his clone. They are so much alike, it's eerie. I just wish Trey didn't have to work out-of-town so much."

"I'm sorry. I'm sure you miss him when he travels. Do you ever go with him?"

"We tried it, but we had to pay for my airfare and that got expensive. Besides, he stays in meetings all day and then takes his work back to the motel at night, so there was nothing for me to do. Not that I cared, but it bothered him to the point that I decided he'd get more done if I stayed home."

Lexie said, "Geez, I'd be afraid to turn that good-looking hunk loose in a strange town, if he was my husband."

"Not Trey. I trust him. We sometimes butt heads, but I know

he loves me and I've never had to worry about him cheating on me."

"It's not him I'd be worried about. It's the crazy women running around who'd make me nervous."

Cami said, "I'm sure Keely has nothing to worry about."

Lexie sighed. "You're right. I'm afraid the time I spent in prison made me question everyone's motives. I need to get past the cynicism and learn to trust people again."

Cami's pulse raced. "Did you say prison? What did you do there?"

Lexie's face reddened. "Oh. I'm sorry. I forgot you wouldn't know." Her eyes welled with water. "I was incarcerated. If you want to back out, I won't blame you."

Cami shrugged. "You aren't getting out of this deal that easily, girlfriend. You're stuck with me."

"Don't you want to know why I was in the pen?"

"Not unless it's a very interesting story. Time's wasting. We have things to do, places to go and people to see."

"Thanks, Cami. We have two possibilities on Schillinger's Road, a couple on Cottage Hill Road and one on Grelot."

"What about your grandparents' apartment?"

She crinkled her nose. "Let's look at it after we've seen the others."

"Fine, but why not first?"

"Even if we should both decide on the garage apartment, I'd feel better if you were given options."

"It sounds like fun to fix it up and I'm sure it would be a comfort to your grandparents to know you were only a few steps away."

"I love them dearly, but whatever you and I decide, we'll decide together. I've learned decisions we make concerning where we work, where we live, or with whom we live, can be very important. One of the best decisions I've ever made, was the day I checked out a Room for Rent sign. Never did I realize how that decision would impact my life. God knew she was exactly what I needed at a time I was at my lowest."

"I suppose you're referring to Bubba's Jewel?"

Lexie snickered. "Bubba's jewel? Absolutely. I can see he's been talking to you, and it doesn't take long to realize he's crazy about that love of his, does it? My pet name for her is Mama J, since she's been a real mother to me. She and Bubba have quite the love story. If it were a novel, it would be too bizarre to be believable."

Cami's lips pressed together in a slight grimace. "I had that kind of love, once." She turned to hide the tears clouding her eyes. "It certainly appears the timing was perfect for everyone."

"Yes. Perfect. I was an emotional wreck when I moved here. I foolishly thought I was in love with someone who was engaged to someone else, so I cried a lot those first few weeks, but Mama J, would sit and listen, then she'd quote a verse from the book of Romans about how things will work together for—"

Cami nodded. "All things work together for good to those who love the Lord and are called according to His purpose."

"Yeah, that's the one. Even when things looked bad for Mama J, she never gave up hope that things would work together for good. Being a widow, she was as lonely as I was. She didn't like to talk about her past—so I didn't pry—but she was a great listener. We'd often stay up until long after midnight, talking. There were times I'd come in from work and she'd have tea and cookies waiting for me. We'd talk for hours, into the night. You might say, she's the mother I never had."

Cami mumbled, "Sounds like the mother I *once* had."

"Oh, I'm sorry, Cami. So, you lost your mother, too?"

She chewed the inside of her cheek, then muttered, "Yeah, I lost her." Clearing her throat, she said, "Time's wasting. Let's get outta here."

After checking out one tiny apartment in a bad neighborhood, one very pricey condo, one fairly decent apartment and a real dump, Cami drove Lexie back to the diner.

Cami said, "So, now that we've seen those, what do you think?"

Lexie weighed her hands in the air. "Frankly, they all were a disappointment. The condo on Grelot was definitely the nicest, but the rent is too steep for my pocketbook. No wonder the price wasn't listed in the ad. I need to get back to work, but if you'll pick me up at the diner in the morning, I'll get the key and we'll go check out the garage apartment."

"Won't Bubba be upset if you leave work again?"

"He won't mind. It's only a couple of miles from the diner, so we won't be gone long. I figure he'll be glad we didn't like what we found."

"Why would you think that?"

"Maw-Maw and Paw-Paw practically raised him, so I think he'd feel better if we were close by to help keep an eye on them."

"That's sweet. He seems like such a gentle soul. I really like Bubba."

Lexie smiled. "He's the best! I'd better get inside to earn my paycheck. See you in the morning."

CHAPTER 15

Bubba rummaged through the morning mail. His hands trembled when he read the name and address on a soiled envelope he held in his hand:

Mandy Gafford, c/o Bubba's Diner
Highway 90, Mobile, Alabama.

His first impulse was to toss it in the trash and never mention it to Keely. His other option would be to give it to her and allow that low-down kidnapper, Wylie Gafford to wound her all over again. The decision wasn't a difficult one. After all, there was no one there by the name of Mandy Gafford. She never existed. That was the name Wylie gave her. It was the name Keely believed for years, to belong to her.

Born Keely Carlton, she was now Keely Carlton Cunningham, happily married and enjoying the family she never knew she had, growing up. Choosing to go with his first impulse, Bubba flung the letter across the room to the waste paper basket. Perfect toss.

If it was the right thing to do, why did he feel like such a heel? Wasn't it his duty to protect his precious niece from the homeless derelict who kidnapped her on her fourth birthday and held her captive for years? Bubba's blood boiled at the thought of the liar who messed with her mind, making her believe he was her father after separating her from her family. Keely admitted she hated the verbal abuse and living on the streets with Wylie, yet she wouldn't admit the grungy old fellow wasn't fit to be alive. Everyone else could see it. Why couldn't she?

Hours of counseling from those who felt it would be emotionally draining for her to see him again, failed to convince Keely that visiting the old goat in prison would be a huge mistake. However, through countless pleadings and bitter tears, she had reluctantly complied.

But now, this . . . he chewed his bottom lip and weighed the consequences of his actions. A letter from the old fellow could be all it would take to send her running straight to him. How she could allow someone who stole her childhood and kept her beat down with his constant insults could still wield such a strong influence over her was beyond Bubba's comprehension. He did the right thing. Hiding the letter from her would be for her own good.

His throat tightened. He pushed his chair back, stood and trudged over to the waste basket. Leaning down, he picked up the envelope. Was he crazy? *Throw it back and forget you ever saw it, Bubba.* He swallowed hard. Was the voice inside him coming from the Holy Spirit . . . or from his own fleshly desire to be Keely's protector and punish this poor-excuse-for-a-human whom he found undeserving of forgiveness?

His gut couldn't have ached worse if he'd swallowed a two-edged sword. All her life, Keely was never allowed to make decisions. Wylie Gafford always made them for her. Bubba hated making the comparison, but wasn't that exactly what he was attempting to do? As much as he hated the idea, he had an obligation to give the letter to her. Didn't he? Or did he?

She'd been doing great lately. The day Wylie went to prison, Trey pleaded with Keely to put the past behind her and it appeared she'd done so. Bubba could only imagine how livid Trey would be—and rightly so—to learn that the sorry so-and-so, Wylie Gafford, was attempting to wedge his way back into Keely's life.

Bubba quickly crammed the envelope into his shirt pocket, when Trey opened the door to the diner.

Trey yelled, "Hey, Bubba. Keely said tell you she'll be in shortly, if you need her."

"No problem. Lexie won't be gone long. Keely's okay, isn't she?"

"You wouldn't think so, if you'd heard her moaning and groaning, just before I left."

Bubba's eyes widened. "Is she pregnant?"

"Pregnant? No, it's much more serious than that."

Bubba swiped his forehead. "What's going on, Trey?"

Trey seemed to enjoy watching Bubba squirm. "Bad hair day, and you know my wife is not gonna leave the house looking less than perfect."

Bubba's low chortle, had a gloomy ring to it. "Is that all? You had me worried."

Trey slapped him on the back. "You worry too much, Bubba. Keely's a big girl now. In spite of her traumatic past, I've been proud of the way she's put it all behind her to become a strong, independent woman."

"Has she Trey?" He motioned to a nearby table. "Have a seat." His voice quaked. "There's something I'd like to run past you before she gets here."

"What's up?"

"Are you quite sure she's put the past behind her?"

"Oh, I'm not saying she's forgotten what she went through growing up, but the good memories seem to slowly be replacing the bad memories."

"Are you nuts, Trey? How can you even suggest there were any good memories?"

Trey wanted to explain he referred to the good memories he and Keely shared, but Bubba flew into an uncharacteristic rage.

"Good memories, my foot. There were none. Poor baby was snatched from her parents by an abusive kidnapper, who used every opportunity to keep her beaten down and under his control." You, of all people, Trey, know the emotional toll she's paid because of the trauma he put her through. I've tried hard not to hate the man."

"I understand what you're saying, Bubba. We all went through trauma, not knowing if she was alive or dead. At seventeen, I fell in love with a girl I thought was named Mandy Gafford, and when she disappeared for seven years, I was devastated. After Wylie Gafford was tried and convicted, I wanted to hate the man. But a wise mentor once told me that hate can destroy a person and I believed him."

Bubba grunted. "Maybe you shouldn't have put too much confidence in that mentor of yours."

"Not true. I've thanked God many times for putting you in my life when I was growing up. As horrible as Keely's life was, she found it in her heart to forgive Wylie and God has allowed her to heal. It was when I realized she was able to forgive him for what he did to her, that I was able to forgive him, also. Do I wish it had never happened? You bet. But for her sake, I'm thankful she was able to put it behind her and move on."

Bubba's heavy breathing exposed his irritation. "Correct me if I'm wrong, but it seems to me you're wanting to excuse Wylie Gafford for what he did to my little niece. I'm sorry, Trey, but I don't feel the scumbag deserves my sympathy. You can go to the prison in Atmore, sit down and chew the fat with him if you want to, but don't expect me to do the same."

"Hey, you're getting all fired up. Slow down and take a deep breath. You apparently misunderstood what I was saying. I'm not defending him. What he did was horrible. If there ever were grounds to hate a person, I suppose you might say Keely had every right to hate him. But who would suffer? Not Wylie. I know most women wouldn't be able to find it in their heart to forgive, but my darling wife is not 'most women.' She's one of a kind."

"I don't get you, Trey. The day they convicted Wylie, you pleaded with her, just as I did, to stay away from that prison. I was proud of you for wanting to protect her."

"You're right, Bubba. When she said in court that she forgave him and would visit him in prison, I was very concerned. But planning to visit the man who controlled her for years is very different from refusing to allow hatred to control her. I still feel it would serve no good for her to see him, although she's much stronger now than when he was first incarcerated."

Bubba leaned across the table, his eyes glaring. "I hope you aren't saying you think she should go running down to Atmore to see the monster."

"No. I'd rather she *never* see him again, but I wouldn't try to stop her. I'd stand by her, because I trust her judgement."

Bubba threw his hands in the air. "Seriously? You're her husband, Trey. I'd hope you'd want to protect her from evil, and you know as well as I do, that man is nothing but pure evil."

Trey threw up his hands. "I don't know why you and I are even having this conversation. It's been over a year and it hasn't come up since the day of the trial.

"But what if it should come up again, Trey? Suppose he tried to wedge his way back into her life by insisting she visit? Wouldn't we have a responsibility to stop her from going?"

Trey's lip curled slightly. "Surely, you jest. We both know that no one is gonna tell Keely what to do. She's her own woman and she'll do whatever she feels is right." He reached over and laid his hand on Bubba's arm. "And can't we both agree that's one of the things we love about her?"

Bubba gave a half shrug. "Frankly, I think she's still vulnerable and needs guidance when it comes to making major decisions, and I wish you could see it, too."

"What brought this up? I don't understand where this is coming from."

Bubba pushed his chair back and stood. "I need to get back in the kitchen. You want pancakes and link sausage this morning?"

"Sounds good. I'll wait until Keely gets here to eat, but she'll only want a couple pieces of toast." Trey picked up a newspaper from off the table.

Bubba walked toward the kitchen, reached in his pocket, and discretely dropped the envelope back where he should've left it the first time he tossed it in the trash.

Lexie and Cami rushed through the door, giggling like a couple of school girls.

Trey said, "You two seem to be in a chipper mood. I hope some of that exuberance will rub off on Bubba."

Lexie's eyes widened. "He's not upset because I'm late, is he?"

"No, he said you'd be coming in late." He stuck his hand out. "I believe you've met my wife, Keely. I'm Trey. And you must be Cami, the girl everyone is talking about." Trey took a sip of coffee. "My dad says he's lucky to have you on his team."

"Dr. Cunningham is the finest in his field. I look forward to working with him."

Lexie whispered. "So, Trey, were you saying Bubba is in a foul mood?"

"He's been a bear this morning. I don't know what his problem is, unless he's getting the wedding jitters."

"Not a chance. Gotta be something else." Lexie pulled out a chair at Trey's table. "Have a seat, Cami. Are you sure all you want is a cup of coffee? Bubba makes wonderful French Toast."

"No thanks. Coffee's fine, but I'll take it to go, please."

"Nonsense. You have nothing to do in that motel room until lunch. Hang out with us until it's time to go."

Cami sat down across the table from Trey, then glanced around the room. "I suppose Keely's in the kitchen?"

"No, she was still fooling with her hair when I left. She'll be in shortly. I have to go to Gulfport this morning and I think she plans on hanging out with you girls while I'm gone."

"Will you be gone overnight?"

"No, thank goodness, this is a day trip, and it's a good thing. I have a feeling that wife of mine is gonna leave me if I keep staying away on these extended trips." He chuckled. "She's accusing me of having a secret girlfriend stashed away somewhere."

Cami swallowed hard. "Do you?"

"Keely's teasing of course, but if I did have, you can bet she'd be a secret. That little wife of mine is as gentle as a kitten when she's happy, but trust me, the wildcat comes out if you cross her."

She recalled Keely's words when she compared her husband with his father. *His son is his clone. They are so much alike, it's eerie.*

Lexie walked over with a cup of coffee and sat it in front of Cami. "Bubba needs me in the kitchen to fill a to-go order. If you change your mind about that French Toast, let me know. It's awesome."

Cami said, "I really should go. I feel like I'm loitering."

Trey said, "Please don't rush off, unless you really need to be somewhere else, of course. Keely gets quite lonely when I'm gone, and I'd feel better if I knew she was spending time with you. It would do her good. Keely didn't grow up here, and I sense she gets quite lonely at times."

"There's nowhere I need to go and I'd love to spend time getting to know her."

"Thanks. You're everything my father said." When he reached across the table and placed his hand on top of Cami's, she instinctively jerked back. Her heart beat like a jackhammer and she could hardly breathe.

His face glowed red. "I apologize. I shouldn't have done that, but I wasn't thinking. I realize you don't know me, but trust me, it was merely a spontaneous reaction—a result of my gratitude, when you agreed to stay for Keely's sake. I'm afraid I offended you and I'm truly sorry. Forgive me?"

"Forget it, so I can." Trey was Dr. Cunningham's son and her remark was snippy. What was she thinking?

"Forgotten." His warm smile meant he hadn't taken offense to her curt response—or either she was right in the beginning and he was coming on to her. She squirmed in her chair.

"I see my beautiful wife pulling up in front of the diner, now."

Keely rushed through the door. "I'm glad you're still here, Trey. Sorry, I'm late. Couldn't do a thing with this mane of mine."

Cami said, "You have beautiful hair. I suppose the curl is natural?"

"A natural headache but I thank you for the compliment. It's good to see you again, Cami. I understand you and Lexie plan to fix up Maw-Maw and Paw-Paw's apartment. How exciting."

She forced a smile. "News travels fast."

Trey shoved his chair back and stood. "You'll learn, Cami, that Maw-Maw gets the news out faster than the Mobile Press." He pecked his wife on the cheek. "Gotta run, babe. You ladies enjoy yourselves and try not to give Bubba a hard time. I don't think he'd be in the mood for it."

Cami's heart sank when Keely's eyes filled with tears as she watched her husband walk out the door. Trouble in Paradise, or was she only imagining things, based on hospital gossip?

CHAPTER 16

Keely ambled over to the coffee warmer in the corner of the diner. She glanced down at the waste basket, just as Bubba started into the kitchen. "Looks like someone forgot to empty the trash last night."

Bubba's face pinched into a frown. When he reached down and snatched up the waste basket, Keely caught a glimpse of her name on a dirty envelope. "Wait, Bubba!"

"Have a seat, Keely. I'll be right back with your toast."

"Forget the toast. I saw my name on something. Looks like a letter."

"It's trash. Now, go sit down."

"That sounds like an order. What's your problem?"

"I'm not the one with a problem." He walked toward the door.

"No, Bubba. I'm serious. There's a letter in there addressed to me. It's probably junk mail, but I'd still like to see it."

"It's nothing you need to see."

"You aren't to be the judge of what I need to see, Bubba Knox. I want my mail." When she grabbed at the wire basket, it toppled and the yellowed envelope tumbled out.

Keely's eyes widened when she picked it up. Clutching it to her chest, she muttered through clenched teeth. "You had no right, Bubba. How many other letters have there been?"

Cami began to understand what Trey meant about the wildcat coming out of the kitten.

Bubba's lip quivered. "Get in the kitchen, Keely, and we'll talk. There's no need to air this in front of others."

"There's nothing to air, Bubba. I received a letter. It has my name on it. You had no right to hide it from me." She tore the envelope open. Her eyes scaled the words on the pages, before she fell back into a seat in a corner booth and bawled.

Cami's imagination went immediately into frantic mode. A Dear John letter? But why would Trey write it, then throw it away? Did he have a change of heart? Or did he give it to Bubba to give to Keely after he left, and Bubba tossed it in the trash? Yes, that had to be what happened. Perhaps she should leave. The less she knew about their marital troubles, the better off she'd be. She stood and grabbed her bag.

Lexie was busy with customers, but she whisked past Cami and quickly whispered, "I don't know what's going on with Keely, but please go to her. I would, but I can't stop."

Cami groaned inwardly. How she wished she'd slipped out sooner, but how could she deny Lexi's urgent request. She lumbered over and slid into the booth with Keely. "I don't mean to intrude, but could you use an impartial ear? I'm told I'm a pretty good listener."

Keely reached for a napkin and dried her face. "I'm sorry you had to see this, Cami. I love my Uncle Bubba, but sometimes he treats me like a child and it makes me so angry I could scream . . . and this time he went way too far in making it his job to protect me. I'll be glad when he's married and has someone besides me to hover over."

"I'm sorry you were hurt, Keely. I wish there was something I could do to ease your pain, but I have no idea what's going on." She reached in her pocket and pulled out a hankie. "Take it. It's wrinkled, but it's clean."

Keely reached out and smiled. "Thanks . . . Maybe there is something you can do. I think Bubba and I could use an outsider who, without prejudice, would see and understand both our positions and convince him he's wrong."

Cami covered her smile with her hand. "And what if by chance, the outsider convinced you that you might be overlooking something, and Bubba could be right?"

"But he's not."

Lexie walked over, holding a tray for a nearby table. She whispered, "Bubba asked me to check on you. Are you okay, Keely?"

Her lip trembled. "Like he cares. No. I'm not okay. I'm furious with him and he knows why."

Lexie glanced at Cami and lifted her shoulders in a shrug, before walking away.

Keely pulled the letter from the envelope. "This letter was from my da—" A tear inched down her cheek. "From the man I grew up, believing to be my father."

"Stepfather, I presume?"

"No. Kidnapper."

Cami's gasp slipped out. "You were kidnapped?"

"Yes, at the State Fair in Mobile on my fourth birthday."

"That's horrible. How long before you were found?"

"Twenty years."

"No way. Did you ever try to escape and go home?"

"I was traumatized and began to believe Wylie really was my father, so I thought home was wherever he took me. We were homeless most of my life, living in shelters, in shady motels or under bridges. I hated my life but couldn't bear to leave him."

"Why not, if you don't mind me asking."

"I don't mind. I know it's hard to understand. But I thought he was my daddy, and it seemed leaving him would be cruel. He needed me. He had no one else."

"Are you saying he was good to you?"

Keely shook her head slowly. "Good to me? How can I explain? There were times when he'd do things that would lead me to believe he really loved me in his own warped way . . . and then other times, he was verbally and physically abusive. I still bear the marks from his belt on my back but his cruel words left even deeper scars than the leather."

"Oh, Keely, I can't imagine what you went through. How did you find out you were kidnapped?"

"My biological mother is Bubba's sister. Wylie and I happened to show up at the Diner one day, when he came to Mobile looking for a job as a roofer. Bubba had a gut-instinct from the first day I walked in with Wylie, that I was his kidnapped niece." Her lip quivered. "I owe him a lot for rescuing me, and if not for him, I would never have met my sweet husband."

"So, where's Wylie now?"

"Prison. I haven't seen him since his trial."

"I wouldn't think you'd want to see him, knowing what he did to you and your family."

Keely's gaze focused on a drop of water on the table. With her index finger, she circled it, around and around, bringing back a memory when Wylie would often do the same thing. How many other mannerisms did she get from him?

Cami waited.

Minutes later, Keely said, "I can answer your question. I wanted to visit him and let him know I've forgiven him."

"But you haven't?"

"No. Bubba and Trey go into tirades if I even suggest going. Until now, I have given in to their demands." She held the letter up. "But no more. I'm going, and when I tell them what else I'm gonna do, they'll try to stop me, but I won't let them. I can't."

"You don't have to tell me, if you'd rather not."

She handed the letter to Cami. "Read it, and I think you'll see why I have to go to the Prison."

Cami unfolded the letter and read:

"My deer Mandy," She paused. "But I thought the letter was to you."

Keely nodded. "It is. Wylie changed my name to Mandy when he kidnapped me. I took my birth name back when I discovered who I was."

"I see." She continued.

"My deer Mandy,

I miss you so much I cry at nite. I spose I oughta say I wish I hadn't stole you from your folks but that would be a lie cause you are the only good thing I ever had in my life. But it was wrong what I done. I was ruff on you and mean but it was how I was raised and I don't know why I beat you cause I loved you very much. I was always skeered you was gonna leave me. But you never turned your back on me like everybody else.

I had to tell you this while I still can. I got bad kidneys and the doctors got me on sumpthin called diealeesis, they say will keep me alive for a spell but I told doc they can stop it cause I'm ready to leave this ol world. I jest had to tell you I'm sorry for being the mean ol cuss I was and if I could do it over, I'd do things different. That's all I got to say.

Wylie Gafford."

Cami laid the letter on the table and blew out a long puff of air. "Oh, m'goodness, Keely, I can understand why you're torn."

"Can you? Do you, really understand, Cami, because I don't think anyone else will. They all want me to write him off, like he was nothing more than a horrid nightmare. But there's something inside me that wants to reach out and let him know that not only has God forgiven him, but that I have, also."

"So what do you plan to do, or have you decided?"

"I've decided, but I can't tell. I don't want to risk having anyone attempting to stop me. For over a year, I've stayed away from visiting Wylie, because of the pressure from Bubba, Trey and my parents. Trey says he supports me in my decisions, but it's not true. Anytime I mention Wylie's name, he goes into a frenzy and tells me all the reasons why I need to put my past behind me. But I'm through allowing others to make decisions for me. This is one time I have to follow my heart."

Cami glanced at her watch. "Wow, it's later than I thought. I need to be at the hospital in twenty minutes."

"Thank you for listening. I'm glad you were here for me. I'll walk you out. Bubba and I need a little separation time to cool off."

CHAPTER 17

Cami strode down the long hospital hall, her knees wobbling every step of the way. She stopped in front of Dr. Cunningham's office door at exactly twelve o'clock and muttered a quick prayer, before knocking.

Confidence had never been a problem with her before, but she couldn't recall ever being so nervous. Not even the first time she sat on the back of Ian's Harley. What she'd anticipated as being her dream job—now left her second-guessing her decision. If she opened her mouth, she feared the hordes of butterflies swarming inside her stomach would fly out. She heard giggling coming from the Nurses Station and turned to see Dianne and Carla watching her.

She swallowed hard, then knocked gently on Dr. Cunningham's door. She jumped and thrust her hand over her chest when the door opened much quicker than she'd expected.

The tall, handsome doctor's face lit up. "Good Morning, Cami. Did I frighten you?"

"Perhaps a little." She feigned a smile.

"Sorry. I didn't mean to scare you." He smiled, revealing a mouth full of perfectly spaced, sparkling white teeth that gleamed against the handsome tanned face.

"I'm on my way to the Cafeteria for lunch. Please join me and we'll go over a few things, and I'll try to answer any questions you may have at this point."

Cami was aware of four eyes glaring in her direction. As she and the doctor walked down the hall, she heard footsteps behind them and didn't have to turn around to know to whom they belonged.

Dr. Cunningham made small talk as they went through the line. "Cami, I realize the job may seem overwhelming in the beginning, but I have every confidence that you are suited for the position, so please don't be afraid to come to me with any concerns you might have. I'll always have time for you."

He was charming. Perhaps too charming.

After Cami left for the hospital, Keely drove around town for over an hour, before deciding to swing by the hospital to see if her father-in-law, Carlos, could spare a few minutes. No one knew Trey better than his father. She'd present him with the two scenarios that she mulled over. (1) If she intended to go to the prison, regardless of Trey's response, should she go without telling him, then seek forgiveness afterward—or (2) Would it be better if she sought Trey's permission, even though she intended to go, regardless of his response?

She passed by the Cafeteria window and saw Carlos sitting at the table with Cami. Disappointed that he wasn't alone, she went through the line, picked up a salad and sweet iced tea, then sat over in a corner, waiting for Cami to leave, so she could talk privately.

"Keely Cunningham, what are you doing sitting over here all by yourself? Mind if we sit with you?" Before she had time to respond, nurses Dianne and Carla were plopping their trays down at her table.

"You're welcome to sit here, but I don't intend to stay long. I just stopped by to talk with Trey's dad, but he's busy at the moment, so I decided to grab a bite while I wait."

Dianne rolled her eyes. "I hope you have all day. He's with *her*. Everyone in the hospital is just sick at the way that little homewrecker has thrown herself at Dr. Cunningham. Men are so naïve."

Keely could hardly breathe. "I don't think I like what you're insinuating."

Carla said, "Dianne isn't insinuating anything. She's flat-out saying what everyone here already knows. Don't tell me you haven't heard?"

Keely jumped up. "Excuse me." She ran out the door and sat in her car for over an hour, trying to think. How could he do that to his family? And to think she had gone to seek marital advice from him. Her face burned. Was that why Cami sashayed over to her table earlier, pretending to be ever so sympathetic, when she simply wanted to find out if Keely had heard the rumors?

Cami left the hospital and after picking up a quart of milk at the grocery, she rode to the paint store to pick up a couple gallons of paint—seafoam—a beachy-looking color which she and Lexie had agreed upon. Her cell phone rang.

Lexie said, "You aren't still at the hospital, are you?"

"No, I stopped by the store and then swung by to pick up the paint."

"Awesome. I can't wait to get started. You do plan to come to the diner for supper, don't you?"

"Not tonight. I thought I'd get carry-out at Lil's Meals while I'm running around and take it back to the apartment to eat."

Lexie groaned. "Trust me, you don't want to do that. That junk's not good for you, but you're the nurse. Why am I telling you what you already know? Bubba has baked chicken, creamed potatoes and butterbeans left over from lunch. Come eat with us."

"You talked me into it. Be there in about twenty-minutes."

CHAPTER 18

Lexie motioned to a booth near the window, when Cami arrived. "Have a seat and I'll turn in your order. You did want today's special, I assume."

"Yes, thank you, with a glass of sweet iced tea. I had lunch with Dr. Cunningham in the Cafeteria, and I was so nervous, I wasn't hungry. I ordered a grilled cheese, but only ate a few bites."

"I promise you won't be hungry when you leave here."

Cami stared out the window for several minutes, then picked up a menu and glanced over the weekly specials. She looked up when a strange man, plopped down in the same booth, in the seat directly across from her.

"Excuse me, ma'am, but you're sitting at my booth."

Her jaw dropped. "I beg your pardon? Your booth?"

"I gather no one informed you. Everyone knows this is my

booth. I have dinner here every evening approximately the same time and always at this table."

Cami pretended to be searching the table with her eyes. "I'm sorry, but you must have the wrong restaurant. I don't see your name on a booth, here, anywhere."

"Really? What name were you searching for?"

Her lips pressed together.

"You weren't looking for my name at all, since you have no idea who I am. Perhaps if you'd known who I am, you would've known this was my booth."

Lexie walked out with Cami's tray.

Cami frowned and gestured with her head at the man sitting across from her. She cupped her hand over her mouth. "Would you mind explaining to the gentlemen that you sat me here?" With her forefinger circling near her ear, she whispered. "A real loony-tune. He seems to think he owns this booth."

Lexie giggled. "He's a riot, isn't he? He's spent enough money here to own the booth, that's for sure. I assume you two have already made the proper introductions? Good evening, Tucker."

"Hi, Lexie. I don't think this woman likes me."

"I'm sure she will when she gets to know you. Bubba has your steak on the grill. It should be out shortly, since all he has to do is plop it down, then pick it up."

The stranger's rude glare confirmed Cami's suspicion that the man was a bully and accustomed to pushing people around.

With his tongue stuck in his cheek, he said, "Told you this was my booth. You heard Lexie. She says I've paid for it."

"That's not exactly what she said. You have a unique way of twisting words." Cami grabbed her tray. "Fine, I'll move."

"Suit yourself." He pulled out his phone and began scrolling.

Her blood boiled. She plopped her tray back on the table and dropped like dead weight on to the bench. "No. This is not right. Why should I be the one to move? I was here first."

He laid his phone on the table and glanced up. "First you're staying, then you're leaving, then you're staying. Are you always this indecisive? Sit down at my booth or go away You remind me of a Mexican jumping bean, bouncing around."

"Sir, you really don't want me to tell you what you remind me of." He grinned as if she'd just paid him a compliment, which irritated her even more.

He said, "I saw you at the hospital today and have to admit, at first glance, I thought you looked sane. But after meeting you tonight, I'm no longer convinced. I called the Psychiatric unit just now, to inquire if anyone was missing from fifth floor. Apparently, you haven't been gone long enough for them to miss you."

"You can keep up the insults. I have no plans to leave. You think you're cute, don't you?"

"It's hard to deny, with women reminding me every day. What about you? You think I'm cute?"

Her voice cracked with tension as she spouted off a string of litanies. "You're an obnoxious, rude, self-centered, egotistical, arrogant, narcissistic jerk."

"Two adjectives would've sufficed. You could've merely called me an obnoxious, arrogant jerk and covered all your bases. But being the indecisive person that you are, I'm sure it was much too difficult to choose from such an imposing list from your vocabulary. Of course, if you find my company to be repulsive, as some do, you might wish to find another table."

"You think I don't know what you're doing? It won't work. If one of us moves, it will be you. I was here first."

"Ah, but remember, it's my booth. Has my name on it. However, being the gentleman that I am, I'm willing to allow you to remain here to enjoy my company. As difficult as it is for you to make decisions, it would be wise if you could come to a speedy conclusion, since your food is getting cold while you haggle."

Lexie walked over holding a piping hot metal plate with a steak and baked potato. "Here ya' go, Tuck. If it doesn't moo, Bubba said he'll send you another one."

He stuck a fork in it and nodded when the juices flowed. "Looks perfect."

Lexie said, "Tucker, you haven't been giving Cami a hard time, have you? Did you introduce yourself?"

He thrust his arm across the table. "Oh, thanks, Lexie. I forgot. I'm Tucker McDowell. And who are you?"

Cami glanced up at Lexie and accepted his hand, though it grieved her to be civil to the barbarian. To refuse would make him the good guy and she'd come off as being rude, childish and . . .

she swallowed hard. That was enough. Rude and childish. She reluctantly extended her hand and shivered when he squeezed it. She said, "Cami Benrey."

"Nice to make your acquaintance Miss Benrey, but please don't cross your arms."

"I beg your pardon?"

"I know what it means when a woman crosses her arms. You're angry, but you don't have to be. I'm not going to insist that you move to another table. You're a friend of Lexie's, so it's okay if you want to join me."

"It's Mrs. Benrey, and if you recall, I didn't join you. You joined me. Remember?"

His face twisted into a frown. "Mrs.? Well, if you're married, why would you purposely sit at a strange man's table?"

"The only thing you've said tonight that has made sense is when you said I'm sitting at a table with a strange man. I've never met anyone quite as strange. I feel like I've landed in the Twilight Zone. You're nuts."

Lexie blurted. "She jokes a lot, Tuck, and she's no longer married. She's a widow. Her husband was killed, going on three years now."

Cami murmured, "Two years and . . . "

"Like I said . . . going on three years."

Picking up his napkin, he carefully unfolded and placed it in his lap. "A widow? That's different. I wouldn't want you sitting at my table if you had a husband. That would be wrong."

"Sir, need I remind you again . . . .. you don't own this table."

"I get it. You're new here, so you wouldn't have known. I forgive you. But I'm sorry about your husband."

"Thank you. I may be new, but it doesn't mean—"

"Stop talking. I want to eat. Bow your head and close your eyes while I ask God's blessings on my food?"

"Fine. But there was no need for the instructions, since I always bow my head and close my eyes when I pray."

"When *you* pray? Oh, my bad. I didn't realize you wanted to pray. Go ahead, but don't make it long."

"No problem. Would you bow your head and close your eyes?"

For the first time since taking his seat, a smile crept across his lips, then turned into full blown laughter. "You're a hoot. Can't be intimidated, can you?"

"Is that you're goal in life? To intimidate women and little children?"

His eyes twinkled when he smiled. "My steak is getting cold while we haggle. So, shall I pray, or do you choose to do so?"

She rolled her eyes. "Go ahead. I think you chose first." Bizarre. There was no other way to describe this idiot's behavior, yet by some strange phenomenon, he had endeared himself to Lexie and Bubba. For their sake and no other reason, she'd put forth a genuine effort to be civil, though it became more difficult with every spoken word.

He folded his hands and prayed. "Lord, we thank you for the

food we are about to eat and pray that it will nourish our bodies and strengthen us that we might better serve you and others. And help this beautiful, lonely lady sitting in my booth to find the peace she seeks. In the name of Jesus Christ, I humbly ask it, Amen."

What a peculiar prayer. How could he pretend to humbly ask anything? The man didn't have an humble bone in his body. And what made him think she wasn't at peace? He was wrong. She cut off a small piece of baked chicken and shoved it into her mouth. The nerve of him to pretend he understood her, when he knew absolutely nothing about her. Everything in her life was working out perfectly. Wasn't it? She picked up her tea glass and took a sip. She'd found the perfect roommate, she had a darling rent-free garage apartment, and had the perfect job at one of the best hospitals around. Cami tried to hide the tears welling in her eyes. He was right. She was lonely. The excruciating ache inside her filled every moment of every day. But how could he know. He couldn't. There was no way. He was guessing.

CHAPTER 19

The long silence at the booth became awkward. Cami squirmed in her chair. "I'm a nurse. What do you do, Mr. McDowell?"

He smiled. "Call me Tucker."

"Fine. What line of work are you in, Tucker?"

"Day in and day out, I look at pictures, evaluate and give recommendations."

"An art critic? Sounds interesting."

He laughed out loud. "Yeah, that's it. I look at pictures and make a determination on what's good and what's not. I see some that are to die for."

He forked a red piece of meat in his mouth, then rolled his eyes in the top of his head and moaned. "Delicious. You should've ordered the Porterhouse."

She glanced at the red juices on his plate and shivered. "If I wanted to bite a live cow, I'd climb on his back and start with his ear."

"Different strokes for different folks, for sure. Frankly, I prefer live cow to a dead chicken."

Cami laid down her fork and motioned for Lexie. "You can take my plate, but I would like a slice of Bubba's coconut pie for dessert."

Lexie placed the ticket on the table and glanced at the food left on Cami's plate. "You hardly ate a thing."

"Not as hungry as I thought."

She had three choices. She could leave the table and allow him to win, keep her seat and continue the snide remarks, or start fresh by making a sincere effort to initiate a polite conversation. She chose the latter. "You mentioned being at the hospital today. I suppose it's none of my business and you're free to say as much . . . but are you ill?"

She thought it disgusting the way he snorted when he laughed. "Your concern is much appreciated, young lady. Truth is, I'm told I'm ill about as many times as I'm reminded that I'm cute. Some say yes, some say no. What's your prognosis?"

"I've concluded you're annoying. Forget I asked. I was merely trying to have a civil conversation."

Cami handed Lexie her credit card, then reached for a pen and wrote her name at the bottom of the check. Conscious of eyes glaring at her hands as she wrote, she laid the pen down. "Excuse me, sir, but I find your staring to be quite rude and none of your business, but if it's that interesting to you, my bill was $8.35."

"Sorry. You're angry aren't you? You crossed your arms. But I eat here every evening, so I knew how much your meal cost. I only wanted to see what method of cursive you use."

"Cursive?" This guy was a lunatic. "It would be English."

He shook his head. "There's not one called English."

If she hadn't been convinced earlier, there was no doubt, now. Totally insane. She tilted her head toward the ceiling and let out a loud sigh.

His phone rang. "Excuse me. I should take this." He took his phone from his pocket. "Hey, doc. Yes . . . yes, I feel fine. Okay, I'm sitting down. GBM?" There was a long pause. "I understand. No need to apologize. How long do I have?" He gasped and rubbed his hand across his eyes. "Seriously? Two weeks is not much time to get my things in order . . . Thank you, Dr. Sears. No, I can do this. I didn't realize it would be so soon, but I'll be ready when it's time for me to go."

Cami's throat tightened. No wonder he was in such a foul mood. *GBM . . . Glioblastoma*? A brain tumor. So that accounted for his bizarre behavior. Overwhelmed by guilt, she wanted to throw up. Poor guy. In the prime of his life, and to be told he possibly had only two weeks to live, had to be a hard pill to swallow.

He reached for his tea and took a sip. "Excuse me for taking the call. I don't make a habit of it during dinner, but it was from a doctor friend of mine."

Her lip quivered. "No need to apologize. I couldn't help overhearing. I'm so sorry."

"You are?"

"Yes. I was rude to you earlier, and it was unforgiveable. I don't know what got into me."

He lifted a shoulder. "If you say you were rude, I'm sure it's true, but I wouldn't say it's unforgiveable."

Cami cut off a piece of pie, but her stomach wrenched. How could she eat, after the way she had treated the poor guy. "Do you have a family?"

"Nope. I'm all alone. Not even a dog to greet me when I go home."

She took a sip of water. "Is there anything I can do to help?"

"You wanna buy me a dog?"

His ability to joke under such trying circumstances made the situation seem even sadder, yet his attempt to stay positive, endeared him to her in a way she would never have imagined when he first approached the booth. Maybe he was trying too hard. Could be, he needed to talk about his situation, instead of keeping it bottled up.

"You're very brave, you know."

"You really think so?"

"I do." She blinked to block the tears welling in her eyes.

"Thanks. I tend to agree with you. Cute, brave . . . and don't forget . . . extremely ill."

Her throat felt as if she'd swallowed a tennis ball. "Yes, you are, and I wish I had known before I acted like such a heel."

"I understand you couldn't have known how brave and ill I was when you chose my booth, but you couldn't help notice I was cute. Am I right?"

Her eyes moistened. She gently laid her hand on his lower arm and gazed into big brown eyes. "You aren't only cute. You're very handsome."

"Why, thank you ma'am, and you're not too bad-looking, yourself. Would you consider going out with me?"

Cami managed a faint smile while weighing his words. Not too bad-looking? His humor was a mite warped, but at least he was attempting to be funny. "I'd be honored to go out with you."

"Great. How about Friday night? I know just the place."

She turned quickly to hide the tear oozing from her eye. "Friday night it is."

Lexie walked up holding a tea pitcher. "I couldn't help overhearing and I'm so excited that you two have hit it off. I thought you would. Just call me Cupid."

He said, "Well, I hate to leave good company, but I need to get back to the hospital."

Cami said, "At this hour?"

"Yep, I only sneaked out for dinner. Can't stand hospital food."

"They let you do that? Come and go as you wish?"

"And how would they stop me? Shoot me? What a waste of bullets that would be, right?"

145

How could she answer such an absurd question?

He held to the door, then turned around. "I forgot to ask. Where do you live?"

"Lexie and I are roommates. We've just moved into a garage apartment back of her grandparents on Pine Bluff."

"Cool. I know the place. Lexie's grandparents are nice folks, although Miz Lorene tries to give me a hard time." He reached for a napkin and took a pen from his pocket. "Why don't you write down the address?"

"I thought you said you knew where it is?"

"I did. Just write your name and the address. Write Mobile, but you don't have to put the zip code."

Was she allowing her empathy to cloud her judgment? Nevertheless, she took the pen and wrote 401 Pine Bluff Drive, Mobile, Alabama, then handed him the napkin.

His forehead wrinkled.

"Something wrong?"

"Spencerian."

"Spence Who?"

"Your penmanship . . . the cursive is Spencerian. I had guessed you to be—" He paused and glared. "Never mind. I'm glad you sat with me. I'll see you Friday night at seven, Mrs. Benrey."

Her heart melted when he winked.

"Please. Call me Cami."

Lexie said, "Cami, you must've made quite an impression on Tucker. Keely says he hasn't dated anyone since moving here four years ago. She and Trey have tried to set him up, but he always refuses to go."

"Four years is a long time for such a handsome guy. Have you ever wondered why?"

"Who can figure Tucker McDowell? He's not only good-looking, but he's funny, generous, honest . . . oh m'goodness, is he ever honest . . . yet, very much loved by everyone at the hospital in spite of his quirky ways. I can't believe he asked you for a date."

"Thanks a lot. And we're friends because . . .?"

"I meant it as a compliment. You're the first girl he's shown an interest in. I Suwannee, he's as peculiar as a three-dollar bill. He's very possessive of this particular booth, to the point it gets hilarious at times. He's been known to insist a customer move if they happen to sit here. I normally go ahead and set it up for him before he arrives, just to insure he doesn't embarrass someone. And don't get him started on the art of writing, unless you have all day."

"Wait! I didn't choose this booth. You purposely sat me here, knowing he'd be coming in, didn't you?"

Lexie giggled. "Guilty as charged. I knew you'd stand up to him and he'd have a difficult time getting you to move. He refuses to sit anywhere else, so he'd have no choice but to share it with you. He's a sweetheart, in spite of his offbeat remarks."

"You sneak. I should be angry at you, you know."

"Maybe. But if it hadn't worked out the way I hoped, you would never have known I set you up." Her face lit up. "It was a long shot, but it turned out even better than I had imagined."

Cami fought back tears. It was evident Lexie had no idea of Tucker's impending death and the reason for the odd remarks, but if he wanted it told, it was his place to tell it. Not hers.

Lexie said, "I love his dry wit, even though I can't always tell if he's kidding. What did the two of you talk about?"

Cami's stomach wrenched as her mind replayed the phone conversation he had with the doctor: *I can do this. I just didn't realize it would be so soon. I'll start right away getting my things in order, so I'll be ready to go when the time comes.* As much as she wanted to share the information with Lexie, it would be inappropriate to repeat a conversation, which wasn't meant for her ears.

Lexie said, "Hello? Anyone manning headquarters?"

"Oh. Sorry. What was it you asked?"

"I asked what you talked about."

"Talked about? Oh . . . you know . . . a little of this and that. Nothing of grave import . . ." She swallowed hard. "Oh, Lexie, he's so . . . so brave. I hope he'll allow me to make up for the snarky way I talked to him when he sat at my . . . at *our* table."

"Wow, girl, you really are smitten. I like Tucker, but to be honest, he can be quite snarky, himself. He has a way of often rubbing people who don't know him the wrong way, but I'm thrilled you two hit it off. I love him to pieces. I can't wait to tell

Keely that Tucker has a girlfriend."

"Whoa! One date doesn't mean we're a couple."

"No, but it's a great start in the right direction."

CHAPTER 20

Trey kissed his wife goodbye Thursday morning, before departing for a three-day Conference in Savannah. "Keely, I still don't understand why you won't come. You're always complaining about being alone, and now, when you have the chance to come with me and spend a fun week-end in Savannah, you balk. What's the deal?"

"Deal? There's no deal. I just decided not to go. You'll be in classes most of the day. I might as well be home alone, as in a hotel alone."

"That's ridiculous. Classes are over at three, and we'll have the remainder of the day and evening to enjoy the sights. Besides, the motel is in the heart of unique little shops. You'll love it."

"I'm not going, Trey, so there's no need in discussing it further."

He stiffened. "Fine! I'm gone." He stomped out of the house

and slammed the door behind him."

She wanted to run after him and tell him about the letter. Tell him what she planned to do. She would have, too, but he'd side with Bubba, and there was no need in further complicating things between them. Trey was angry when he left. She could only imagine his fury if he learned she was sneaking off to see Wylie.

Sneaking? Why should she have to sneak? She was a grown woman. Why did she feel she needed approval? Growing up with Wylie, she was never allowed to make decisions. When he said go, they went. When he said stay, they stayed. Well, she was stronger, now. Didn't need anyone telling her what she could or should do.

Grabbing the packed bag hidden under her bed, she ran to her car, threw it on the rear seat, and was on her way to Holman Correctional Facility in Atmore, Alabama.

****

Jackie Gorham opened the door to the closet in the bedroom that Lexie had occupied for the past six months.

How she could've become so attached to a young woman whom she'd known for such a short time, baffled her. One thing for sure, Lexie had been a Godsend. Although no one could take the place of her missing daughter—her sweet Camille—Lexie's presence had helped Jackie from dwelling on it 24/7.

However, today the terrifying memories returned with a vengeance. Was her mother-in-law, right? Was she responsible for Jacob's death? Jackie fell across the bed and squalled until her eyes burned from the hot tears, as she recalled every squalid detail of her husband's last night, as if it were replaying in slow motion before her eyes: It was around one a.m., that fateful morning when Jacob staggered into the house—placing it a day after Camille's 21st birthday.

"Where've you been, Jacob? Yesterday was our daughter's birthday and you promised to go with me to place a wreath on her memorial."

"None of your business where I've been, woman. Leave me alone. I'm tired."

"I'm your wife, Jacob. That makes it my business."

"My wife? Get real. You've never been a wife to me, Jackie. I don't even know why you married me."

"You know why I married you. The same reason you married me. You raped me, Jacob. Raped me! When I discovered I was pregnant, our parents forced this on us. But I've never been unfaithful to you. Never."

"You can stop the ruse, Jackie. I've known from the first day I laid eyes on her in the hospital nursery,"

"Known? Known what?"

"Camille . . . Camille had red hair. Her hair changed later, but it was definitely red when she was born. How stupid do you think I am, Jackie? No one in my family has red hair. Mama reminded me that Bubba Knox's hair was almost carrot-colored when he was in elementary school."

"Jacob. I know you don't really believe what you're inferring."

"Inferring? I'm saying it, Jackie. You think I didn't know why you doted on her the way you did?"

"Jacob! You know she's yours. Bubba and I were never intimate, but I'm sure you know that."

Jackie remembered how he picked up the empty flask from the sofa and slung it across the room, while spewing a string of obscenities. It was then he admitted the real reason for his drunken stupor and it had nothing to do with their daughter. He'd been caught embezzling funds from the firm and would be facing prison. Chills ran down her spine, when she recalled finding his lifeless body on the floor the next morning, with an empty bottle of pills near his hand.

Losing their home and all their holdings was hard, but nothing could compare to the heartache of losing her only daughter. Jackie packed up and left Virginia to move back to her childhood home in Mobile, Alabama, left her by her deceased parents. The family attorney in Virginia promised to notify her if Camille should return, looking for her. It never happened. Now, Jackie was convinced it never would.

Camille was last seen almost three years ago, hitchhiking. She was believed to have been murdered . . . by everyone except Jackie. There was even a TV movie made, based on her disappearance. According to the story, a known rapist who had recently escaped from prison, stopped and picked up the beautiful hitchhiker. He was murdered by a gang, before he could be brought in for questioning. The movie ended with police searching the woods for a body.

Jackie refused to believe it. Camille would never have gotten into the car with a stranger. Yet, she couldn't explain why three different people gave statements they saw her hitchhiking the day she disappeared. They were wrong. It couldn't have been Camille. She was smarter than that.

Jackie held on to hope like a drowning woman holds on to a life jacket Today, with a heavy heart she watched her life preserver slowly float down the river, leaving her with nothing to hold to. It was over. Camille would not be coming home. Ever!

Someone banged on the front door, jarring her from the morbid memories. Jackie jumped from the bed and attempted to dry her face with the back of her hand. Taking a quick glance in the mirror, she groaned at the sight of her swollen eyes. "Hold on. I'm coming."

Rubbing make-up over her red face, then straightening her skirt, she heard Bubba's voice.

"Jackie? Jackie! Open the door! Are you okay?"

She unlocked the door and fell into his arms.

"Oh, sweetheart. What's happened?"

"My baby . . . my baby's dead, Bubba."

Bubba walked her to the sofa, cradling her in his arms. "Oh, honey, I am so sorry."

"I think I've known all along, but I couldn't face the truth."

"Honey, it tears me up to see you hurting like this. I wish there was something I could say to make it easier for you. I want to comfort you, but I have no words." Tears seeped from his eyes.

"Just hold me, darling. Don't ever let me go. Promise me . . . promise me you'll never leave me."

"It's a promise." He wanted to remind her that she was the one who left him, years ago. True, her parents were set on having their daughter married to Senator Gorham's son, but did she really have to go? If only she'd trusted him enough to tell him what happened, he would've married her in a heartbeat. How confident was he that Jackie didn't weigh the differences in being married to a high school senior with a part-time job versus a college grad with the means to give her a comfortable life? Bubba attempted to dismiss the haunting thoughts. She loved him and only him. Always had. Or had she? She never discussed her life with Jacob. What if he was wrong? She lived with the man for over twenty years. Perhaps she had to marry him, but if it was rape, would she have stayed? A bitter taste rose from the pit of his stomach.

"Bubba, thank you."

"For what?"

"For being my rock. I've always been able to count on you."

That's me. Reliable ol' Bubba. He brushed a lock of hair from her face. The lump in his throat swelled. "I only wish you'd counted on me when you left Alabama to marry Jacob."

She sat up and glared into his eyes. "Oh, you know why I did what I did. Let's don't go there."

"Sorry." She was right. Rehashing the past could only stir up strife for them both. There were some things he'd be better off not knowing. The only thing he was sure of was his love for her, and he could only hope that she loved him half as much.

After several minutes of silence, he said, "Jackie, are you set on having a wedding ceremony?"

Her lip curled at the edge. "Don't tell me you're getting cold feet."

"Of course not. You know I want to marry you. I'm saying I don't want to wait. I don't care about all the hoopla. I just want us to be together. Forever."

She lifted her head from his shoulder. "I don't want to wait, either, sweetheart, but Keely has gone to too much trouble for us to cancel. It's only one more week."

She was right, of course. With his arm wrapped around her, he pulled her close and kissed her on the forehead. "This is gonna be the longest week of my life."

"You know, I didn't want to come back here, after Jacob died."

So, he was right? He'd wanted to believe she returned because she was still in love with him. His love had been forever. Apparently, it was out of sight, out of mind, for Jackie. He groaned.

"Did you say something?"

"No." He clamped his lips together. Maybe she fell out of love with him, but wasn't it enough that she loved him now? Not Jacob. But him. For the sake of their marriage, he had to bury the painful past. But could he really forget?

"Bubba, you're one-in-a-million. You never grill me about my life in Virginia. Some things are still too painful to discuss, yet I understand it would only be natural for you to be curious. One day, I hope I can share everything."

She was right. He did have questions. For beginners, how did she receive the news that her daughter was dead? Had the body been found? Was it positively identified? If so, did the police relay the information in person? Heaven forbid that she may have heard it on the National news. Or did an ex in-law in Virginia call to inform her? Jackie didn't mention a memorial service. Surely, she'd want to plan one. If only he could've been with her today when she received the dreadful news. He could only imagine how terrible it must've been for her to be alone.

He'd wait for the answers. When she was comfortable talking about it, she'd tell him.

Jackie reached up and kissed Bubba on the neck. Despite all the heartaches she'd endured for the past twenty-four years, Bubba Knox had become the shining light at the end of the long tunnel. Ashamed that he'd caught her having a meltdown, she made a silent vow to be strong for his sake. He was such a softie. She knew how much it hurt him to see her in pain.

Jackie sucked in a lungful of air, then slowly exhaled. She'd denied the truth for too long. Camille was gone and there was nothing that either she or Bubba could do to bring her back. If

Jackie lived to be a hundred, she'd never get over losing her baby girl, but for Bubba's sake as well as her own, she'd make a real effort to remember only the good memories. As much as it hurt, it was time to let go.

CHAPTER 21

The garage apartment was larger than it appeared from the outside and reminded Cami of a gingerbread cottage out of a fairytale book. Though the décor hadn't been updated since mid-fifties, the homey atmosphere made it a fun place to come back to at the end of the day. Her favorite room was the kitchen with its yellow gingham-checked wallpaper.

The two bedrooms—one with a full bed, the other with twins—had a Jack and Jill Bath separating them. Lexie and Cami agreed it would be more fun to share a room, where they could talk late into the night.

After painting the living room and hallway, they were exhausted and crawled into their respective beds at twelve-fifteen.

Minutes later, Cami whispered. "Hey, you awake?"

"Yes. I think I'm too tired to sleep, but I feel good about all we accomplished tonight."

"We did, and the apartment's looking great. I'm glad you're my roomie, Lex. It almost feels like we're kids again, having a slumber party, doesn't it?"

"I don't know. I've never been to a slumber party."

"Really? Never?"

"Oh, I was invited to several, but my stepmother refused to let me go. She did anything she could to make my life miserable."

"That's a bummer. I'm so sorry."

"Don't be. It's all in the past. The best thing she ever did for me was to falsely accuse me of stealing her car. She did it to get rid of me, but as it turned out, she saved my life. After serving time, I came here, found my grandparents and fell in love with Jamal, the sweetest guy in the whole world."

"Lexie, I can't wait to get to know him. I met him briefly at the diner, before he left. He's a very nice-looking man."

"I miss him so much, but he'll only be working the construction job in Georgia until school resumes in the fall. This is his last year, and he'll finally get the degree he's worked so hard for. Jamal is dyslexic, and I'm so proud of how he's stuck it out in spite of the difficulties."

Cami didn't realize how long Lexie talked about Jamal after she stopped listening—not that she intentionally tuned her out, but her mind took over and without meaning to, her thoughts focused on her new boss.

"You haven't heard a word I've said, have you?"

Cami pressed her lips together. "Not true. You said Jamal was dyslexic. See? I did hear you."

"That was fifteen minutes ago. What's wrong, Cami? I feel like you've wanted to say something, but you always stop before you get it out. If I've done something to offend you, please tell me, so I can correct it."

"It's not you, Lex. I don't know if I should mention it."

"Now you have no choice, girl. I won't sleep a wink until you tell me."

Though they were alone, Cami whispered, as if they were in a crowded room. "Lexie, how well do you know my boss?"

"Dr. Cunningham? I've never had an occasion to spend much time around him, but I hear he's a great doctor, and everyone who knows him is crazy about him." She giggled. "And he's not bad on the eyes, either, is he?"

"No. No, he isn't. It's getting late. I suppose we'd better get to sleep or we won't feel like getting up in the morning."

"Oh, no you don't. You can't leave me hanging. What's going on?"

Cami sucked in a heavy breath. "I'm not sure. Please don't say a word to anyone."

Lexie threw her legs off the side of the bed and sat up. "Okay. What's on your mind? Spill it, girl."

"Hospital gossip has it that he's a real Romeo."

"What? That's absurd. No way. I don't believe it. He's Keely's father-in-law, and she adores him. In fact, according to her, the man's a Saint."

"Well, I wouldn't expect his family to know. It's not something a married man discusses around the family dinner table, although hospital employees appear to be privy to his little rendezvous."

"No. Not Dr. Cunningham. Oh, m'goodness, you're serious, aren't you? That's really what they're saying? Cami, I know you wouldn't buy into malicious gossip unless he'd given you reason to think it's true." She groaned. "This literally makes me sick. He's a pillar in his church. What has he done to make you believe the rumors?

"Nothing big. I mean . . . well, it's just little things he's said. I thought nothing of his off-hand remarks at the time, but when added to what the nurses are saying, I've begun to question his motives."

"What motives?"

"Well, the day of my interview, he smiled and told me I was even prettier than my picture."

"Oh, Cami. Is that all? I don't mean to make light of what you're saying, but the truth is, you are very pretty, and for a man to pay you a nice compliment doesn't mean he wants to seduce you. I Suwannee, it's the culture we live in. Frankly, I'm flattered when a man pays me a compliment, although I'm sure I receive far less than you, so I savor each one."

"I get what you're saying, Lex, and I'll admit, I didn't think anything about it at the time."

"So you're saying more came later?"

"I think so."

"You *think?* I don't understand."

"Well, there were nurses who suggested the only reason I was hired was because of my looks. In referring to my job, one of them said the duties Dr. Cunningham had in mind for me would have nothing to do with baths and bedpans—"

"So? That's not a bad thing, is it?"

"But she didn't end it there. She said his duties wouldn't include baths and bedpans for *patients.*"

"Call me dense, but I still don't know why that makes him a sex predator."

"Don't you get it? She was clearly suggesting the baths would be for *him.*"

"Oh, Cami, I really think you're reading too much into this, but I understand. You've heard some idle gossip and it's made you nervous."

"I know you think I'm being paranoid, Lexie, but there's more. As soon as I arrived at the hospital today, he insisted I go eat with him."

"Oh? He insisted?"

"Well . . . maybe insisted is too strong, but he was waiting for me at the door and it was evident he expected me to go with him."

"And where did he take you?"

"We went to the Cafeteria."

Lexie snickered "The Hospital Cafeteria? Sorry, but I don't

think that qualifies as a date."

Cami bristled. "Go ahead and laugh. I understand why you want to defend him. Keely's led you to believe he's this wonderful man who can do no wrong, and I wish with all my heart that I could believe it. But all the attention he's given me makes the rumors appear to be true."

"I'm not trying to defend him. Just saying I'd hate for you to let innocent inuendoes build up in your head, which might affect the way you view your job. I know how excited you were that you landed this position. But I'm listening. Did anything else happen that you've failed to mention?"

"No, I don't suppose . . ." She snapped her fingers. "Wait! Yes. One nurse slipped and called him by his first name. She was noticeably embarrassed and quickly corrected, but she and her friend shared a good laugh, and I realized it was an unintentional slipup."

"Don't you think they jokingly call him by his first name behind his back?"

"I might except—"

"Except what?"

During my interview, Dr. Cunningham, hummed and hawed, as if there was something he needed to say, but had trouble putting it into words. I was taken aback, because he didn't appear to be a man who'd have trouble expressing himself. When he finally got the words out, he said, "It's embarrassing to have to bring it up, Cami, but I should warn you."

"Well? Don't stop. What was the warning?"

"I don't know." He stammered, then said, "Forget it. If it becomes a problem, we'll deal with it."

"So you still don't know what he meant?"

"Oh, I know, alright. It wasn't hard to figure after hearing the insinuations from the nurses. It became obvious he was hiding something that he'd rather I not know. I've met his kind before. I have a very troubling feeling about this job, Lexie. I don't want to leave it, but neither do I want to work for a man who possibly hired me for all the wrong reasons. I don't know what to do."

"Sheesh, Cami. I've tried to defend him, but I'll have to admit, when you put it all together it doesn't sound good. Poor Keely. She'll be devastated if she finds out. She thinks Dr. Cunningham can do no wrong."

"Not only is it disgusting, it's sad. The family is always the last to know."

CHAPTER 22

The seconds ticked off slowly. Minutes seemed like hours as Keely waited behind iron bars for the guard to bring in Wylie.

The woman in the chair beside her was crying while the man on the other side of the window tried desperately to comfort her. He asked about the kids, and she assured him they missed him greatly. He tried to convince her it was time for her to divorce him and get on with her life, though Keely was quite sure the woman meant it when she said it would never happen. They seemed like such a nice couple. How did he wind up behind bars?

She tried to put herself in the woman's place and knew she'd never leave Trey if they were in the same situation. Sure, they had their spats, but she loved him dearly, and he loved her. Her throat tightened. She was about to put him to the test. Keely could only imagine what he'd say when he discovered why she didn't go to

Savannah with him. But Trey wasn't the only one who would've tried to stop her. Bubba would've gone ballistic if he'd known of her plans.

Her heart lurched when she looked up to see Wylie being led into the room by a prison guard. He looked much older. His shoulders stooped, and he walked with an unsteady gait. His skin was pale, his eyes dull.

"Hi Mandy."

Mandy? She didn't correct him. Why should she? She'd been Mandy to Wylie for more years than she'd been called Keely. It sounded right, coming from his lips. He looked so thin. So broken. Had prison done this to him, or was he sicker than she'd wanted to believe? "Hi, Wylie. You've lost weight."

He simply nodded. "You look good, sugar." Tears seeped from his eyes, but he made no attempt to dry his leathery face.

"I got your letter, Daddy." She swallowed hard. There was no need to tell him how she came about getting it.

His lip quivered. "Don't sugar."

"Don't? What did I do?"

"Don't call me that no more. I got no right."

"You never minded before, whether I called you Wylie or Daddy."

"Oh, sugar, that's where you be wrong. My heart swelled every time you called me that word. You ain't got no way o' knowing how I wish I coulda been yo' daddy. But a sorry, good-for-nothing, lazy bum like me could never have had a fine daughter like you. So it's not fittin' for you to call me nothing but by the name my mama gave me. It's the onliest thing in this world that belongs to me."

The knot in her throat became too hard to swallow. Raw emotions swung like a pendulum from one extreme to the other.

He leaned in. "I wrote you a 'hunnerd' times or more, sugar, but I tore 'em all up. Figured I had no right. When I found out I was gonna die, I just couldn't leave without telling you how sorry I am for what I done to you. I know it didn't seem like it to you, 'cause I didn't know how to show it, but truth is, I loved you more'n I've ever loved anybody or anything."

Anger rose from the pit of her stomach, hearing the words she longed to hear as a child. "You *loved* me? Wylie, how can you say you loved me? Remember how many times you told me I was not a keeper? Just a trash fish? And the time you took me away to keep me from seeing Trey? I remember your exact words. You said, 'That ol' boy doesn't love you. It's as much fun to pull in a trash-fish as it is to pull in a bream, but at the end of the day, the bream is the Keeper, and the trash-fish is thrown back into the cold waters.' You said, 'When that ol' boy gets ready to pick him a wife, he won't be taking you home to meet his mama.' Wylie, that was not only not true—it was cruel. You *never* loved me. If you had, you couldn't have said those horrible things to me."

"That's where you be wrong, again, sugar. I wanted you to believe nobody else would want you, but me, so you wouldn't leave me. Crazy, I know, but I 'spect we both have known for a long time that I'm more'n a bit crazy." He wrung his hands together. "Well, sugar, I reckon that's all I got to say. Thank you for coming, but no need for you to come back no more. I done said all I needed to say. God speed."

God speed? Strange parting words from a man who had always dared her to mention anything that had to do with religion. "Wylie, I've talked to your doctor, and I want to be tested."

"Tested? You got sumpin' wrong with you, sugar?"

"No. I mean tested to see if I'm a match."

"I still don't get your drift. Ain't you married already? Why you be looking for a match? Ain't he good to you?"

"Yes, he's very good to me. That's not what I'm saying. You need a kidney. I have one I don't need. If we're a match, I can give you one of my kidneys."

"Are you loco? Ain't gonna happen. No way. That's the stupidest idea I ever heard tale of. I ain't about to take one of yo' kidneys." He threw up his hands. "You can make up your mind to forget that stupid idea. I won't do it."

"Yes, you will! Without a donor, you can't live. I may not be a match, but I won't sit back and let you die if it's in my power to give you what you need."

Wylie jumped up and motioned for the guard. "Get me outta here. I don't wanna see her in here again." He turned and shook his finger in her face. "Go home, Mandy. I don't want nothing from you. You hear what I'm saying, girlie? You think I want a kidney from a cotton-pickin' trash-fish? You ain't got nothin I want.

Nothing! And don't you never come back here again." He was still ranting when the guard led him out of the room.

Keely walked out in the hallway, deflated but not defeated. She met Wylie's doctor in the hall.

He stopped. "Mrs. Cunningham! I'm glad I ran into you. Did my nurse get in touch with you?"

"No. Why? Are the results back?"

He gave a thumb's up. "Congratulations. It looks like you're a match. I hope you've had time to read the information I gave you."

"Yessir, I did."

"Good. We're not at the finish line yet, by any means. You'll need to undergo a couple more tests, but if it turns out the tissue is compatible and the CT scan looks good, then the transplant surgeon will go over everything and get it all set up."

"Fantastic."

"Are you sure about wanting to do this, young lady?"

"Why would you ask? It's my understanding I don't need both my kidneys and Wylie needs one to live."

"Even though we do transplants on a regular basis with great results, you do understand there are risks to any surgery."

"You've sufficiently covered the risks, and I understand. You aren't trying to talk me out of it, are you doctor?"

"No, but I can't help wondering about your motive."

"My motive? Isn't wanting to help a dying man, motive enough?"

He crossed his arms over his chest. "I've heard a little of Wylie's story and it's my understanding that he kidnapped you and robbed you of your childhood."

She nodded. "True."

"So, help me understand why you'd want to reach out to a man who ruined your life, by giving him his life?"

"You aren't the only one who will want answers to that question. It's true, I had a hard life growing up with Wylie, and there were many times I wanted to run away. Leave him."

"But you didn't. Why not?"

"I couldn't. As much as I wanted things to be different, I believed Wylie to be my father. Don't you see? I couldn't desert him then . . . and I can't desert him now. For years—for better or worse—he was the only father I knew. I *never* liked him. He was rude, crude, abusive and humiliated me—but I know now that even though I didn't like him—I loved him and in his strange, unorthodox way, I really believe he loved me, too."

The doctor was paged and Keely went directly to the office of the transplant surgeon for further instructions, then hurried back to the motel to check out.

CHAPTER 23

Cami's Friday night date went much smoother than she'd imagined. Due to Tucker's charming wit, she was able to forget—at least for a short while—that his days were numbered. He appeared to enjoy the evening as much as she did. That is, until the server handed him the check.

Tucker took a quick glance, then pushed it across the table. "You pay this time, and if we decide we want to do this again, maybe I'll pay next time."

She shoved it back. "You are so funny."

"I don't mean to be." He stood. "Oh, and don't forget to leave a tip. The service was good, didn't you think? You should always tip when the service is good. Trey says I should tip even if I don't like the service, but I think that's stupid."

Cami's smile faded. With her thumb and finger, she twisted the faux pearl ring on her right hand—a nervous habit. "Are you serious? You seriously expect me to pick up the tab?"

Confusion painted his face. He stammered. "Uh . . . No. Of course not." He grabbed the check and pulled out his wallet. "I asked you on a date. That means I should pay. Right?"

"Exactly."

He paid with cash and left a generous tip on the table, which confused her even more, since she'd reasoned he was chintzy. If only she had known him before the brain tumor. It was difficult to know if his odd behavior was simply his personality, or whether it was disease progression.

"That was fun, Cami. I like you. I like you a lot. I could marry someone like you."

She laughed out loud. "That sounded like a proposal."

"Maybe. But Trey says I should count to twenty before making an impulsive decision. One . . . two . . . three . . ."

"You can stop counting. I've been married once and I don't plan on doing it again."

"That's okay. I don't mind. We don't have to get married."

Was he attempting to be funny? Perhaps it was the meds. She tried to think of a subtle way to find the answer. "Tucker, I don't mean to pry, but when I have a lot on my mind and am on medication, it's sometimes easy to forget to take it. And sometimes I may not remember if I've taken it at all and take it twice. Does this ever happen to you?"

"Oh, that's not good, Cami. Not good at all. You're autistic, aren't you?"

Cami stiffened. "Autistic? No! Why would you ask such a question?"

"I could tell. It was impossible not to notice the stimming during dinner tonight. Did you know you twisted your ring twenty-two times? Twenty-two! You hardly had time to pick up your fork, before you'd lay it down and give your ring a twist." He focused on her hands. "Uh . . . Twenty-three."

She looked down at her fingers and quickly placed her hands under the table. "You're kidding. You didn't actually count—"

"I did. And you turned your tea glass a quarter-turn, without picking it up, fourteen times."

Cami's pulse raced. *Stimming? Me?* One of them had a real problem. Now, to figure out if it was him . . . or her.

****

Keely drove to the airport to pick up Trey. She jumped out of the car when she spotted him waiting out front. She rushed toward him with open arms. "Trey, I am so sorry about the way . . ."

He planted his lips on hers, making it impossible for her to finish the sentence. "You have nothing to apologize for, honey. I had no right to make you feel guilty for not wanting to go with me."

He placed his luggage in the back of the vehicle, then walked around to the driver's side.

A few miles from the airport, Keely pointed to the Seafood Haven. "I'm hungry. Why don't we stop here for lunch?"

"Great choice. I missed you, babe." He was full of talk at the table. He stopped in mid-sentence. "Hey, I haven't stopped yakking since we sat down. I want to hear about you. What happened while I was gone?"

"Nothing much." Her lips pressed together. She had never lied to Trey.

"Nothing?"

The way he repeated the word made her nervous. It was as if he knew and was waiting for her to admit it.

"Well, that's not completely true."

"Oh? So what did you do to occupy your time?"

She dropped her head and mumbled. "I went to the prison."

He leaned forward. "I don't think I heard you. What did you say you did?"

"You heard right. I went to the prison."

"Why, for Heaven's sake?"

"I think you know why. To see Wylie, of course."

Trey's face turned red. "Oh, Keely. We've talked about this."

"No. You talked about it. I listened."

"Apparently, you didn't listen very well, or you wouldn't have done such a stupid thing."

"So I'm stupid, am I?"

"That's not what I said."

"I'm ready to go, Trey."

"You haven't finished your shrimp."

"I'm suddenly not hungry."

Trey slammed money on the table, they stomped out, got into the car, and neither spoke a word on the ride home.

CHAPTER 24

When Cami arrived at work, Monday morning, she was relieved to discover Dianne and Carla had been assigned the night shift. The atmosphere was much more relaxed when those two weren't around. Dr. Cunningham invited her to sit with him at the Cafeteria, and it was a relief not having to glance over her shoulder to see four eyes glaring in their direction.

He said, "Camille, now that you've had an opportunity to see how things operate here at Trinity Hospital, have we grown on you?"

The question caused shivers down her spine. "I love my job, if that's what you're asking, Dr. Cunningham."

"I'm glad. But that wasn't exactly what I was getting at. There are a couple of nurses who can be quite hostile to new employees. They literally ran off my last nurse. I'm hoping you're strong enough to ignore their jealousy."

Cami didn't have time to think before the fiery words spewed from her lips. "They have no reason to be jealous of me. It's *your* reputation—not mine—that's at stake, doctor. I was hired as a nurse, and that's the only duties I intend to perform, so if I was hired for any other reason, you can fire me now."

His face flushed. "I beg your pardon?"

"I'm privy to the hospital gossip and I'm not competing for you."

"Competing? For *me*? Camille, I have no idea what you're talking about. There are a couple of nurses who have been here for years and seem to think they should be elevated to positions they aren't qualified to fill. My last nurse was apparently too insecure to handle their jabs. But I don't see you as being an insecure person."

" Are you serious? You really don't know?"

His jaw tightened. "Apparently, I don't."

"They're saying there's a little hanky-panky going on and that I was hired to be your next playmate. What you do is your business, but in the event there's truth to the gossip, I'd like to be upfront and let you know I'm not throwing my name in the ring. I'm a nurse. Not any man's mistress."

He ran his hands through his thick, curly locks and glared. "Are you through?"

She swallowed hard. "Yessir." What made her continue with such a long diatribe? She may as well clean out her locker after lunch. She'd just kissed a good job goodbye. So be it.

"Camille, Let me assure you, I'm a happily married man. I have a beautiful, precious wife that I look forward to going home to at night. There's nothing more important to me than my Lord, my family, my country and finally my profession. I would do nothing to jeopardize any of them." He reared back in his chair and groaned. "Tell me something. Have I ever been anything less than professional with you?"

She lifted a shoulder.

His brow arched in disbelief. "Yikes! You seem to think I have. Please. Tell me what I've said or done to make you feel uncomfortable. We need to straighten this out now."

She lowered her head.. "You . . . you said I was prettier than my picture?"

"My word. And you took that as a come-on? Sheesh, when did it get to the point a man can't compliment a lady? So, you were offended because I noticed you were pretty? If that troubles you, I'd suggest you stop wearing make-up, don't fix your hair, take less pride in your attire and maybe . . . just maybe no one will notice that you're an attractive young lady." He rubbed the back of his neck and lowered his voice. "Sorry. I shouldn't have said that. It's so humiliating, though, to think that you could've assumed I was interested in having a romantic interlude because I said you were pretty. Obviously, you haven't seen my wife, or you'd realize I have no reason to look outside my own home. I've yet to find a woman who looks half as good, present company included."

Heat warmed her face. "I considered it a harmless

compliment—in the beginning."

"In the *beginning*? But, now, after-the-fact, you're saying you've decided to second-guess my intentions? Why?"

"It was after I heard the talk that—"

His gaze met hers, as he waited for her to complete the sentence.

She'd gone this far. No need to hold back now. "The word on the hall is that you choose female employees based on looks and not on resumes. Their derogatory remarks about me were highly insulting."

His jaw jutted forward. "Dianne and Carla. So, that's what they're saying?"

She nodded.

"I'd like you to fill out a formal complaint. Will you do this?"

"No sir."

"Why not?"

"I'd rather turn in my resignation than to get involved in a squabble that could hurt my chances of landing another position in another hospital."

"I'd like to say I understand, but at the moment, I'm having difficulty understanding a lot of things." He pushed his chair back and glanced at his watch. "I suppose we should get back to the office. I'm expecting a Conference call in ten minutes. If you're afraid of me, I'll understand if you choose to walk several paces behind me."

Her throat tightened. He was angry. But why should he be

angry with her? He asked for the truth, didn't he? She chewed the inside of her cheek. No. He didn't ask. She blurted it out. All he said was he hoped she was not as insecure as his former nurse. What made the volatile words spew from her mouth?

Cami wanted to believe Dr. Cunningham. But if he was the adulterous womanizer the nurses accused him of being, wouldn't he deny it with his whole being, knowing the consequences? And what about his son? Like father, like son, they said, referring to Trey. Keely made no secret that she was bothered by her husband's constant out-of-town trips. Perhaps she had more reason to be upset than she wanted to admit.

CHAPTER 25

Thursday evening, Cami went straight to the diner after work and sat in Tucker's booth, hoping he'd show up. She buried her face in a book when Keely walked toward her. Not that she didn't enjoy Keely's company, because she did. Just not tonight. And not in Tucker's booth.

Keely said, "Hi, Cami. You're just the person I wanted to see." Cami grimaced when she sat her iced tea on the table and slid into the booth. "How's that good-looking father-in-law of mine treating you?"

Her heart hammered. Was she being sarcastic? Maybe Dr. Cunningham had a good laugh when he discovered she thought he was coming on to her and decided to share it with his family. Cami stiffened. "He's not *treating* me. I'm not his patient."

"Cami, I know why you're so defensive, but you shouldn't be, because there's nothing to the rumors."

Her back stiffened. "I gather from your remark that your father-in-law told you of our conversation."

"He did, but only after I approached him with what I'd heard. He was livid when I told him what Dianne and Carla were saying. Trust me, anyone at the hospital can tell you there's never been a finer husband, father, doctor, or Godlier man than Carlos Cunningham. He knew a couple of nurses were jealous you got the job they applied for. He'd been afraid they'd give you a hard time. He said he almost warned you of their vindictiveness when you arrived, although he had no idea how malicious they really were. Both nurses have been given their walking papers. It seems they were behind other nefarious goings on at the hospital, that finally came to light when Dad questioned other employees.

Cami said, "I suppose I can kiss my job goodbye, and I won't blame him. I bought into the rumors and allowed my imagination to run wild. I feel awful for believing the accusations."

"You can stop worrying. Dad's fine. He was upset at first, but he's calmed down and realizes where you were coming from."

"That's a relief. And I owe you an apology, also."

Keely said, "All is forgotten. I hope you'll stay here and keep me company while I wait on that husband of mine. He's having dinner with a client, but said he'd meet me here for dessert after they finish. He's crazy about Bubba's coconut pie. I only wish he was as crazy about me."

"I beg your pardon?"

"Trey's not too happy with me at the moment." The corner of

her lip lifted. "Aww, don't look so worried. He'll get over it. Married life has it's perils, but also its pearls. I love him and he knows it, even if he does make me want to bite ten-penny nails in half, sometimes." She glanced out the window. "Uh, Cami, would you mind if we moved to another table? There's someone coming, who—"

Cami shook her head. "Actually, I prefer sitting at this one." She looked up and smiled, when Tucker walked in. He slid in the seat next to Cami and took her hand. "Hello, beautiful."

Keely's eyes widened. "What? You two are acquainted?"

Cami said, "Yes. Lexie didn't tell you?"

"No. Bubba has kept her busy, so we've barely had time to say hello. So, this is why I couldn't get you to move to another table. Why didn't you tell me?"

Tucker grinned. "She likes me. That's why she didn't move."

Cami said, "That's ridiculous. I wanted to read, and the light's better here."

"Not true, and you know it. You like me. Tell her about us."

Keely rocked her head back and forth from Tucker to Cami. "This gets more interesting with every passing minute."

Cami rolled her eyes. "There is no us."

Tucker draped his arm around her in a teasing fashion. "Not so. We're dating."

Keely had just taken a swallow of tea, and covered her mouth to keep from spitting it across the table. "You? Dating? Now, I know you're joking."

Cami giggled. "Actually, he's telling the truth about dating. He's taking me to an exclusive restaurant, next week. And he'll be paying. Again."

Tucker's eyes squinted into tiny slits. "Exclusive is her word, not mine. I have a little hot dog shack in mind." He patted Cami across the back. "You'll love it, kiddo."

Trey walked up, slid in the booth beside his wife, then pecked her on the cheek. A big smile spread across his face. "Tucker, I see you've met our friend, Cami."

"Yeah, I like Cami, Trey. She's cool. Pretty, too. Don't you think she's pretty?" His eyes widened and he immediately pushed out an open palm. "Oops. I wasn't supposed to ask that, was I? You're married."

"It's okay, Tuck. I'm married, but not blind, and you're right. She's very pretty."

Cami blushed. Tucker sounded so . . . so childlike. From their first meeting, she'd been taken aback by his lack of filters, but she chalked it up to extreme arrogance, having little regard for what others might think of his bizarre remarks. She was a nurse, for crying out loud. Why didn't she pick up on the signs? With the brain tumor in its last stages, it was a miracle he could still put sentences together. She thought back to their first date and realized she accepted out of compassion, but she'd come to enjoy his company, in spite of his quirky ways. He possessed a sweet innocence that she found surprisingly attractive. Cami couldn't help wonder what it would've been like to have known him before—before the GBM. She could only imagine that he must've been a real charmer.

Keely said, "Tucker, have you invited Cami to the wedding?"

"Oh, yeah. The wedding. When is it?"

"Didn't you get your invitation?"

"I did, but I can't remember."

"October 3rd. Trey and I would be happy for you two to double with us."

"Like a double-date?"

"Exactly." Keely glanced at her husband and winked.

Cami fought back tears. What sweet friends.

Tucker gave a thumb's up. "Sure. I'd like that."

Trey said, "Well, buddy, shouldn't you ask her if she'd like to go?"

"She would. I know she would. The food will be better than at the Hot Dog Shack and even cheaper."

Cami said, "You're right. I'd love to go to the wedding with you."

Tucker reached across the table to high-five Trey. "Told you."

CHAPTER 26

Keely rolled over and turned out the light. Trey hadn't mentioned the argument or asked her anything about Wylie. No doubt, he'd had time to realize how wrong he was.

She slid over in bed and laid her head on his chest. "Still mad at me?"

He draped his arm around her. "You know I can't stay upset with you."

"I'm glad. I thought after you had time to think about it, you'd realize I was doing the right thing. I don't think I could live with myself if I let Wylie die, knowing I might could've helped him."

"Honey, you do know that it's not your fault that Wylie is dying. There's nothing you can do about it."

"There may be."

"What do you mean?"

"I'm being tested as a kidney donor, and so far, it's looking good. I'm a match."

"WHAT? "Keely, have you completely lost your mind? That's the craziest thing I've ever heard of. No way. What you're suggesting is downright wrong for a dozen different reasons." He pulled back and crossed his arms over his chest.

"I'm not suggesting anything, Trey. I'm telling you my plans. Wylie won't live unless he has a donor and I may hold the key to his life inside my body. How could I not do this?"

"Get real, Keely. You don't owe Wylie Gafford diddly squat. It burns me up, every time I think of how he ruined your life."

"Ruined it? If he hadn't brought me to Mobile when I was seventeen, we would never have met. We should thank him for that."

"That's ridiculous and you know it. I suppose you've forgotten how he snatched you away in the middle of the night and kept you hidden for years, when he found out about us."

Keely's stored-up emotions released in uncontrollable sobs.

Trey rolled over and draped his arm around his wife, pulling her close. "Hey, hon, I'm sorry. Please don't cry. I shouldn't have flown off the handle the way I did. Forgive me?"

Still snubbing, she dried her face with the top sheet.

"You have such a tender heart, sweetheart. That's one of the things I admire about you. But it's that soft heart of yours that can skew your ability to think straight at times. You want to save the world, and it's not your responsibility."

She couldn't believe what she was hearing. "Are you saying I can't think for myself? That I need someone much smarter than me to make my decisions for me? Someone like you?"

"Now, you're purposely twisting my words. You know that's not what I said."

"Then what is it you're saying, Trey, because it sounded to me as if you were forbidding me to save Wylie."

"Forbid is a strong word. But if it will stop you from proceeding with this outlandish idea of yours, then call it what you will."

"I'm meeting with the transplant surgeon tomorrow."

"Keely, have you considered how an operation such as this might affect your having a child?"

"Becoming a kidney donor is not the way a woman gets pregnant, Trey. Having a husband home at nights is how most women become pregnant."

"Now, you're being mean. I was asking if you've considered the risks? I have a job that takes me away at times, but if you remember, I tried to get you to go with me on my last trip, but you refused."

"And now you know why."

"Yeah. I know. Wylie Gafford has suddenly become more important to you than your husband." He jumped out of bed, grabbed his pillow and headed for the sofa in the den.

Keely tossed and turned all night. A part of her wanted to go wake her husband and apologize for harsh words spoken. The other part reminded her that she hadn't changed her mind and knowing Trey, he hadn't changed his.

When the alarm went off, she jumped out of bed. She wouldn't mention it if he didn't. They'd eat breakfast, he'd go to the office and she'd keep her appointment in Atmore. They both had expressed their thoughts on the subject and she saw no reason to discuss it further. By now, he'd had time to cool off and would come to understand she was doing the Christian thing. It wasn't as if he wasn't a very caring, compassionate man. He was. He loved her with all his heart and was concerned about her own health. She could appreciate that. Couldn't she? After all, she'd been told of the risks involved.

She draped a robe around her, combed her hair and dabbed a little make-up on, before going into the den to wake her husband.

He was gone. All the rage from the night before, returned. How could he be so unreasonable? Did he honestly think she needed his permission to give a kidney? If she wanted to give away all ten fingers, they were her fingers. Sometimes he acted as if he owned her.

A note was stuck on the refrigerator. *"Keely, the consulting firm, Heartz & Heartz contacted me yesterday about contracting with them on a huge account. I turned it down because it would require me to work from their office in Orlando, from three to six months. However, I realized tonight how silly it was for me not to take it. I wanted to spend more time at home, but I now understand that you don't need me around. I'm not sure you ever did. I love you, Keely, and I always will, but I don't like the direction our marriage is heading. I'll be praying for the surgery to go well for you. All my love, Trey."*

Tears blurred her vision. If he really loved her, he would've supported her in her decision instead of being hard-headed and deserting her when she needed him most.

She dressed and headed up 65 N. to Holman's Prison in Atmore.

CHAPTER 27

"Tucker, if you really care for Camille, you should tell her."

"Who's Camille?"

Carlos Cunningham threw up his hands. "Isn't that who we were discussing?"

Tucker heaved a deep sigh. "I thought you were keeping up, doc. I was talking about my girlfriend. Cami Benrey."

"Okay. Gotcha. We're talking about the same girl. I suppose her friends refer to her by the nickname, Cami, but she goes by Camille at the hospital. She's very bright, Tuck, and I can certainly understand why you'd be interested. But I believe you should be upfront with her and let her know you are aware that you have a problem."

"You can't be serious, Carlos. I came to you because I need you to help me, not to get instructions on how to sabotage the relationship. Been there, done that in high school. Swore I'd never make the same mistake again."

"Mind telling me what happened?"

"I've always known I was different. When I was little, kids in the neighborhood would tell me they weren't allowed to play with me. I became a loner—not because I wanted to, but I couldn't keep friends. I was never invited to parties, not even birthday parties. My mother was afraid I didn't like girls, but she was wrong. Girls didn't like me. Mom kept pushing me to ask a girl out, so my senior year, I made her a promise, and I asked the prettiest girl in the class to the Prom."

"Good for you."

"No. Not good. She laughed in my face. Called me a doofas. I didn't know what a doofas was, but I knew it wasn't a compliment. I became the laughing stock of the senior class, and that was the first and the last time I ever asked a girl for a date. Then, I met Cami. She's different. Sweet. She laughs at me, but it's not the same. She doesn't act like I'm a doofas. I love her, Carlos. I think I'll tell her that when I see her. She's the girl I want to marry."

"Whoa. Take it slow, buddy. If you move too fast, you could scare her off."

"But I'm afraid if I don't ask her, some other guy will make a move and I'll lose her. I really think she likes me, and I don't want to mess up."

"Then let her know."

"I thought you said don't tell her."

193

"I meant don't tell her of your plans to marry. But tell her you have Asperger's. She's a nurse, Tucker. She'll understand."

"Uh-uh. No way."

"I thought you came to me for advice."

"I did, but I expected you to tell me what to do to keep from messing up. In therapy, I'm told to watch for body language. If she smiles, it's good. If she crosses her arms, that's bad. But how do I know if she really likes me?"

"If she didn't like you, she wouldn't continue to go out with you."

"Yeah?" His smile widened. "We've had nine dates. Ten if you count the first time she sat at my booth."

"That's a sign she enjoys your company, so tell her. Please. You're a brilliant doctor, Tucker. Asperger's doesn't define you."

"Easy for you to say. Try telling that to the last two hospitals that let me go because of it."

"But you learned from those experiences. Right?"

"Yeah, I learned people don't want to hear the truth, even when they say they do. Like the old hag who came into my office and asked me to refer her to a plastic surgeon. He plunked his hands on his hips and mimicking a feminine voice, he said, 'Tell me the truth, doc, do you think it would be a waste of money for me to have the wrinkles around my eyes removed?'" Tucker threw his hands in the air. "Now, Carlos, would you please explain to me why she'd preface it with 'tell me the truth,' and then report me when I gave her what she asked for?"

"What did you tell her?"

"The truth. I told her it's not the wrinkles folks see when they look at her. It's that Jimmy Durante snout of hers. If she'd asked me if she needed a nose job, I would've understood her concern. But a few lines around her eyes? Sheesh, that was the least of her problems."

Carlos covered his smile with his hand. "Tucker, the expression 'honest to a fault,' describes you. People don't always need to hear the truth, the whole truth and nothing but the truth. Your trouble is in discerning what to tell and when. That's why I'm encouraging you to be honest with Cami, so when you do say something inappropriate, she'll understand and can put it in the right context. She's not only a great nurse, but I've found her to be very compassionate."

"So, you're saying if I tell her, she'll pity me. I don't want her sympathy."

"No, that's not what I'm saying. I'm saying, she'll learn to ignore any inappropriate responses if she's aware where they're coming from. She obviously likes you. You say you've had nine dates, already, and she's agreed to go with you to the wedding? Sounds as if it might be getting serious."

"Yeah. She wouldn't want to go with me if she didn't like me. Would she?"

"That's true."

"So, if she likes me, why would I want to tell her and risk running her off?"

"If you don't tell her, you're more likely to run her off, Tuck. She needs to understand that in spite of all your many great qualities—and trust me, you'd be a fine catch for any woman— you sometimes have a real problem communicating. Would you like for me to tell her?"

"No! If anyone tells it, it should be me."

"Fine. But the sooner the better."

"I'll think about it."

"Changing the subject, but I hear you're gonna speak at the Memphis Conference."

"Yeah, there was no way I could refuse. I owe Dr. Sears a favor and he had a speaker to bail on him. I've only had a couple of weeks to rearrange my schedule, but he's come through for me on several occasions, so I couldn't say no."

"What's the topic?"

"GBM. I'll have a forty-five-minute session before lunch and another forty-five-minute session after lunch."

"So you'll only be gone one day?"

"True. I'll fly up there that morning and be back home by nightfall." Tucker glanced at his watch. "Thanks for your time, Carlos. I need to get back up to the lab."

Cami bumped into him as he was walking out the door. Her eyes widened. "Tucker? I . . .I didn't expect to see you here."

He looked over his shoulder at Dr. Cunningham. "Uh, I didn't expect to see you here, either."

"I work here, Tucker. I'm Dr. Cunningham's nurse."

"I know that. We're still going out Friday, night, aren't we?"

"I'm looking forward to it. You did say we'd go to The Riverwalk Restaurant, didn't you?"

"Yep. It's expensive, but I know you'll like it. I plan to wear my blue suit. I hope you'll wear something nice. Sometimes I run into people I know, there."

Cami glanced over in time to see Dr. Cunningham's eyes roll in the back of his head, as if he were embarrassed for her.

"You'll look very handsome in your blue suit, and I'll wear my best dress. I want to make you proud."

Tucker's broad smile made her want to run over and wrap her arms around his neck. What a sweet, brave man.

CHAPTER 28

Keely went straight to the Hospital. After waiting in the transplant surgeon's office for over two hours, she was called to a back room and sat up on the examining table, where she waited another forty-five minutes. She straightened her back when the doctor finally entered the room.

"Mrs. Cunningham, I'm afraid I have some good news and some bad news. The good news is that you aren't a candidate—"

Her jaw dropped. "No. That's not good news. It can't be right." She bit her lip to keep from crying. "Why, doctor? Is it because Wylie got upset? If that's it, I'll talk to him. I can get him to understand. That's it, isn't it? He's convinced you that he doesn't want me to do it. But I'm a match. Right? So, go ahead and set up the surgery."

"That's impossible, Mrs. Cunningham. Not in your condition."

"My condition? There's nothing wrong with me."

"You're pregnant."

"I'm what?" She placed her hand over her mouth to muffle the scream. "No way. You can't be serious."

"I'm very serious."

Her breath came out in spurts. "You're absolutely sure?"

"One hundred percent."

"Oh m'goodness, I'm gonna have a baby. Unbelievable. That truly is good news and bad news. I'm thrilled to learn I'm pregnant, but what about the surgery? Can Wylie wait that long for a kidney? Nine months is a long time, as sick as he is."

"That's the bad news." He dropped his gaze. "I'm sorry to inform you that Mr. Gafford succumbed this morning at three a.m."

Keely burst into tears. "Are you saying Wylie . . . Wylie's . . . *dead?*"

The doctor pulled a letter from his pocket. "He left this for you."

The tears blurred her eyes, as she silently read the scrawled penmanship.

"Dear Mandy,

If you're reading this, I'll be in Glory or on my way. Not sure how long it takes to get there. That's sumpin I forgot to ask the Chaplain. But all I could think about after you left me was you must love me, else why would you give a part of yourself so I could live. Didn't rightly make sense. I bawled like a baby that night, and the guard thought I was dying then and there. He sent for the Chaplain. We talked 'til wee hours of the morning, and finally, I understood what you tried to tell me so many times. In spite of my mean, ornery ways, Jesus loved me and was willing to give his life for sorry ol' me. Chaplain said he reckon you was a lot like Jesus.

I know you mean well and I don't want you thinking I ain't obliged by your offer, but I'm ready to walk on them streets of gold. I love you, sugar. I don't reckon I've ever said that to nobody. I shoulda said it to you a long time ago."

Daddy

She wiped the tears from her face, and a little chuckle turned into full-blown laughter.

"Mrs. Cunningham suppose you lie down on the table. I can see this has come as an emotional shock. Would you like for me to call your husband to come be with you?"

"My husband? Oh, yes, my husband. He needs to know."

"Do we have his phone number in our files?"

"No." She slid off the table and stood. "I'm sorry, but I must go, now. I need to find my husband."

"Mrs. Cunningham, you've gone through a terrible shock. For your sake and the baby's, I'd prefer you not leave until you've had an opportunity to absorb the news. I'll have my nurse call Mr. Cunningham." He pursed his lips You wouldn't happen to be related to Dr. Carlos Cunningham, would you?"

"He's my father-in-law. I need to get in touch with my husband."

"Are you sure you're okay?"

"I've never been as okay as I am now. It's not just okay. It's wonderful. Wylie is a believer. Oh, m'goodness, how precious is that? Not only that, but he told me he loved me, doc. You can't imagine how many years I longed to hear him say that. And if that wasn't enough good news for one day, Trey and I are gonna have a baby. How much better can it get?" She grabbed her purse from off a nearby chair and hurried out the door.

When she reached the car, she pulled her phone from her purse and looked up the number of Hearst & Hearst. "Hello . . . This is Mrs. Trey Cunningham speaking and I need to talk to my husband."

"Mrs. Cunningham, your husband hasn't arrived."

"He hasn't? What time do you expect him?"

"I'm not sure. He called and talked to Mr. Joseph Hearst, but Joe is out of the office and I don't expect him back this afternoon. If your husband comes in, would you like for me to have him return your call?"

"Yes. Yes, please. Tell him it's urgent. I need to speak with him."

"Yes ma'am. I'll relay the message."

****

"Trey, honey, come in. You look like you haven't slept in days. What's going on?"

"Mom, I've blown it."

"Come in and let's sit down at the kitchen table and tell me what it is you think you've blown."

Mary Jo Cunningham poured two cups of coffee and sat down across the table from her son.

"My marriage."

"That I can't believe. I know how much you love Keely and how much she loves you. Did you two have a lover's spat?"

"I wish that's all it was." Trey poured his heart out, beginning by explaining Keely's avoidance to reason. "Mom, why in the world would she want to put her own life in jeopardy for someone who mentally abused her for years, in an effort to keep her under his sorry ol' thumb? He couldn't care less if she lives through the surgery, but I care. The man's not fit to live."

"To begin with, Trey, people become kidney donors every day. But I don't think that's what this is about. I can't believe you mean what you're saying."

"You're right. I didn't. I've said a lot of things lately, that I didn't mean." His Adam's apple bobbed. "I don't know what's wrong with me Mom, but I'm afraid I've lost Keely because of stupid things I said to her." After Trey finished pouring out his heart, he said, "I called Joe this morning and turned down the job. I wouldn't be worth a hill of beans to the firm, with me down there and Keely here. I want to go home but I'm sure she doesn't want to see me and I can't blame her. Frankly, I don't want to be around me, either."

Mary Jo sat quietly, gazing into her son's eyes.

Trey shifted his gaze. "Mom, you and Dad have the kind of

marriage, I want. Trouble is, I'm not the man that Dad is. I wish I was."

"Trey, do you really want a marriage like ours? Because if you do, I can tell you the secret."

"Please!"

"The Bible says a husband should love his wife as Christ loves the church, and that a wife is to be submissive to her husband." She lifted her hands, palms out. "That's it. Pretty simple."

"Ha! That might've worked back in Jesus' day, but I don't see it working today."

"It works for us, Trey."

"But you and Dad talk things out. Keely doesn't listen to me."

"Trey, you're being defensive. Marriage is not a football game. It's not offense and defense. It's more like a see-saw."

"Did you say see-saw?"

"Yes. The only way to lift up your partner is for you to be willing to go down. When a wife understands her husband's heart's desire is to raise her up, it causes her to want to do the same for him and the see-saw begins to operate as God intended."

"I think I get it, Mom." He raked his hands through his hair, then pulled out his cell phone. "Excuse me. I need to call my wife."

He stuck the phone back in his pocket. "She's not there."

****

Trey drove to his home and before he reached the door, Keely came running outside and jumped into his arms.

"Keely, I am so sorry. I didn't—"

She planted her lips on his, blocking the words from escaping. "I'm so glad you'll be here to go with me to the wedding tomorrow night."

"I never intended to miss Bubba's wedding, but I wasn't sure you'd want to go with me."

"Don't be silly. Trey, I went to the hospital and the doctor—"

"About that, Keely. I was wrong. When Bubba told me that Wylie had sent you a letter, I bragged to him about how I trusted you to do the right thing; yet, when you were faced with a decision, I didn't support you. I'm so sorry, baby, that you couldn't count on me to lift you up when you needed me most."

She slid from his arms. "Let's go inside. I have something incredible to tell you."

Once inside, she plopped down on the couch, cross-legged. "How much time do we have?"

"What do you mean?"

"When do you have to be in Orlando? I thought you'd already be there."

"I turned it down." He reached for her hand. "When's the surgery?"

"There won't be a surgery."

"Oh, Keely, I was wrong. I want you to go through with it . . . for Wylie's sake. I'll be there to support you both. I promise." He was surprised he could say it and mean it, yet he did.

She whispered, "Wylie's dead, Trey."

He slid his hand across his face. "Dead? Oh, babe, I'm so sorry."

"I have something I want you to read." She pulled a folded paper from her pocket. "I went to Atmore, hoping to set up the surgery but when I arrived the doctor informed me Wylie was gone. Then he gave me this letter."

Tears puddled in his eyes as Trey read the scribbling. His voice was barely audible. "This is awesome. The seeds you planted took root, sweetheart. I was such an idiot. How did I wind up with such a sweet—"

Keely put her hand over his mouth. "Wylie's salvation is only part of my wonderful news. I couldn't have donated a kidney, even if Wylie hadn't died. We're pregnant, Trey."

"No way! You're teasing, right? Oh, Keely, babe, are you for real? Pregnant?"

"For real. We're gonna have a baby, sweetheart."

CHAPTER 29

Cami pulled the new dress from the garment bag. "What d'ya think, Lex?"

"Wow. It's gorgeous."

Cami smiled. "Gorgeous, yes, but is it *nice*?"

"Uh . . . nice?"

"Yeah. We're going to the Riverwalk and Tucker requested that I wear something nice." She giggled.

Lexie's mouth flew open. "No! Please tell me he didn't say that. Oh, Cami. I hope he didn't hurt your feelings. I love Tucker, but he can say the weirdest things."

"My feelings weren't hurt." She held the yellow dress in front of her and gazed in the mirror. "I love it. I hope Tucker likes it."

"He should. I saw the price tag. You really like him, don't you?"

"I care for him."

"That's what I meant. You care for him. A lot. I can tell. And I'm glad. Tucker needs a woman in his life."

Her lip quivered. "I only wish I'd known him before—"

Lexie said, "Before? So you know? About his condition, I mean."

"Only because I overheard a phone conversation. But I didn't know you knew. Why didn't you tell me, Lex?"

"I wanted to, Cami, but I was sworn to secrecy. Keely and Trey are Tucker's closest friends, and the only reason Keely told me was because Tucker said something inappropriate to me one night and hurt my feelings. I didn't want to serve him after that. So, Keely explained to me that he wasn't responsible for some of the things that come out of his mouth. But please, don't let it go any further. I wouldn't want Keely to think I broke a confidence."

****

The night was perfect. The restaurant was situated on Mobile Bay, and the server sat them at a remote table in the corner, by the window. The Fisherman's Platter was superb, especially the fried oysters. Tucker's dark eyes sparkled. If he had a little girl, would she inherit her daddy's big brown eyes? Would a little boy get Tucker's handsome looks?

"What are you thinking?"

Cami blinked to keep the tears from falling. Tucker would make a great dad, yet he'd never have the opportunity. So sad.

"You didn't like your dinner, did you?"

"The dinner was delicious. When the server gets back with your credit card, let's take a walk on the pier."

The waiter handed Tucker the receipt. "Sign here, sir."

Tucker signed his name, then handed it back to the young man, along with a folded paper napkin. "Would you be so kind as to sign my napkin?"

He patted his chest. "Me, sir? You want my autograph? You must have me confused with someone else."

"Maybe. Are you the waiter that works at the Riverwalk?

Cami buried her face in her hands.

"Yessir."

"Fine. See, I don't have you confused."

"But why would you want my autograph?"

"Do you mind?"

"I guess not." He took the pen and scribbled, "Jeff Waite."

Tucker's face twisted into a frown and he slid the napkin for Cami to see. "That's D'Nealian."

The waiter grabbed the napkin, read what he'd written, then laid it back down. "No sir. I'm Jeff Waite. I knew you mistook me for someone else."

"I take it you aren't familiar with Donald Thurber?"

"Never heard of either of those guys. I was pretty sure you had me confused when you asked for my autograph."

Cami, whispered, "Let's go, Tucker. We planned to walk the pier. Remember?"

He wadded up the napkin. "Your penmanship is atrocious,

young man. But I'm not blaming you. I blame Donald Thurber. He's the one who dumbed down the exquisite Spencerian cursive. He claimed, of all things, that it was too difficult for kids, and it made their hands tired. How lame is that for an excuse to be lazy?"

"Not sure, sir, but I'll take your word for it." The young man glanced around. "Uh . . . excuse me. I have other tables to wait."

Cami shoved her chair back. "Tucker, what is this obsession you have with penmanship? That was very embarrassing, not only for him, but for me, also."

"Embarrassing? Why would you think that? I'm sure the kid appreciated having an opportunity to learn something new."

"No. No, he didn't appreciate it and neither did I! People don't care if you approve of the way they write. Why can't you understand? That's the third time you've stopped someone when I was with you, to chat about the origins of the various forms of cursive. Trust me, that is of no interest to anyone but you."

"I'm sorry. I didn't mean to embarrass you, Cami. I'll try to do better."

"Try? You don't have to try. Just stop it."

"Your arms are crossed over your midsection. You're angry."

Her hands dropped to her side. "I'm *not* angry."

"You may not know it, but you are. It's not cold in here, so I'm positive you're angry."

She sucked in a lungful of air and slowly exhaled. "Okay, maybe I did get a little frustrated, but I'm over it. It was no big deal and I overreacted. Let's not let it ruin an almost perfect night."

She grabbed him by the hand. "Come on. Let's take that moonlight walk on the Pier."

Cami's heart ached. She'd blown it again. She wasn't angry at Tucker. She was angry at herself for becoming so attached to someone else who would leave her. This wasn't supposed to happen.

CHAPTER 30

Lexie was ecstatic that Jamal was coming home, and the diner would be closed for a week, giving her more time to spend with the man she loved.

Cami answered the door. "Come in, Jamal. I'm Cami."

"We met at Bubba's Diner. Remember?"

"That's right, we did."

He wrung his hands and glanced around the corner.

Cami smiled. "She'll be down shortly."

A shrill shriek came from upstairs, and Lexie bounded down the steps with open arms. "Jamal, baby!"

"Wow! Look at you. You're even more gorgeous than when I left. Turn around and let me take a good look. What a babe."

Lexie grinned and obliged by twisting around, allowing the skirt to her lavender bridesmaid's dress to swirl. She said, "We need to hurry. Keely wants the wedding party there early."

Cami paced the floor, watching the clock. Where was Tucker? Her imagination worked overtime, conjuring up all sorts of horrible scenarios.

When Keely and Trey came, she insisted they go on to the church, to keep from being late.

Keely said, "Trey and I will be sitting on the groom's side, since Bubba's my uncle. We'll save you and Tucker a seat."

At five-twenty, she heard a car pull up. She grabbed her purse and hurried to the door.

Tucker said, "Where's Keely and Trey. Shouldn't they be here by now?"

"They came earlier, but I told them we'd meet them there."

"Sorry I'm late. I couldn't get away from the hospital before now. I like your dress. It's nice."

"So you were at the hospital this afternoon? Running tests, I suppose?" If only he'd open up and tell her about the tumor.

"Consulting with doctors, mostly. I spend more time at that place than I do at home, but I think we can still make it to the wedding on time. You look nice. Very pretty. Did I say that already?"

"You did. Thanks." It didn't matter that he wasn't as demonstrative as Jamal with his compliments. 'Nice,' and 'pretty,' worked just fine.

"Thank you, Tucker. You're very handsome, tonight."

"Tonight?"

She smiled. "I should've added, 'as always.'"

"So you do think I'm handsome?"

"Of course, you are."

"Would you marry me if I asked you?"

Was he joking? How could she be sure? "You're being funny, right?"

"Nope. Dead serious. Well, not dead. But serious."

Chills ran down her arms. "Do you want to get married?"

He laughed. "I think the guy is supposed to do the proposing."

"I wasn't proposing, silly. I think you did."

"No, I didn't. But if I wanted to propose, I'd probably pick you."

She rubbed her hand across the back of her neck. "Thanks. I think."

"But you wouldn't marry me, Cami, if you knew the truth about me."

Her pulse raced. "How can you be so sure?"

"I'm sure."

"So what's wrong with you, Tucker?" She flinched when he appeared agitated.

"Why are we hanging around wasting time? Let's go."

"Sure." She locked the door behind them. "Tucker, would you like for me to drive?"

"Cool. That's a great idea."

Relieved, Cami walked toward his car and opened the door to

the driver's side.

"Hey, what are you doing?"

"You said I could drive. Did you change your mind?"

"No. I want to ride on the back of your bike. I've never ridden on a motorcycle."

She swallowed hard, thinking of the hours she took, fooling with her hair. He was already standing beside her bike, grinning like a little boy on Christmas morning. How could she deny him? What if this was his last opportunity and she refused. She'd never be able to forgive herself. "Fine. Hop on."

"Aren't you gonna wear a helmet?"

"No. It's only a couple of blocks to the church, and we'll travel the backroads."

They arrived at the church with only minutes to spare. She could only imagine what her hair must look like. *Apple Annie.* Rydetha's words echoed in her ears.

"Li'l Darling!" A big man getting off a bike, threw up his hand.

"Cross T!"

Tucker said, "You know those bikers?"

"Sure do. Come over and let me introduce you." After making the proper introductions, she said, "Where are you guys headed?"

"We have a fund-raiser for a fellow biker who's been diagnosed with an inoperable brain tumor. He has a wife and two small kiddos. Sad situation. We'll be gathering at the Pier in Fairhope and from there, we'll ride to Jacksonville to visit him at the clinic."

"Awesome! If I wasn't so crazy about my job at the hospital, I'd be riding with you."

Tucker said, "You say he has a brain tumor? He's lucky to have friends like you."

Cami bit her lip. Until now, she'd not considered his financial situation. If only he'd drop the façade and admit the truth to her.

The ushers motioned for them to hurry inside. The heavy doors closed behind them, and the preacher approached the front of the church.

Responding to Keely's hand motions, the young groomsman ushered them down the aisle to the third pew.

The bikers sat in the back of the church.

Keely leaned over and whispered. "You look beautiful, Cami."

"Thank you. So do you."

"I'm so excited. I've never seen Bubba looking so happy. They've been in love for over twenty-years, you know."

"Really?" Cami giggled. "What was the problem? Bubba have cold feet?"

"Sad story. She got pregnant in high school and left town." The music began and Keely sat upright in her seat. "I'll explain later."

Cami remembered her own wedding and wondered what it would've been like to have had a beautiful service such as this one, with bridesmaids and the works.

The bridal march began and the bride entered through the

double doors, wearing a pale blue suit and a large-brimmed hat, which dipped in the front, covering half her face. Everyone stood and turned toward the back of the church. There was something about the way she carried herself that reminded Cami of her mother. Peculiar how much the man escorting her favored— Cami's eyes squinted into tiny slits. *Uncle Johnny?*

The bride stopped in the middle of the aisle, looked up and squealed. "Camille!"

Seeing the bride's face for the first time, Cami clamped her hands to either side of her head and screamed. "No, no, no!" She scrambled over Tucker's feet, dashed past the bride and shot out the door.

Jackie kicked off her six-inch heels and ran after her, but Cami jumped on the bike and sped away.

Bubba raced outside and grabbed Jackie in his arms. "What just happened?"

"Didn't you see her? That was my daughter. She was here."

"No, sweetheart. The girl who ran out is a young widow who moved here from Tennessee. I'm afraid we just witnessed a nervous breakdown. I suppose hearing the wedding march was too painful for her. There's a room full of people waiting inside. Come on back into the church. After the wedding, I'll send someone to find her."

"I'm sorry, Bubba. I can't. Camille's alive and is obviously confused. Please, help me find her."

"Hon, I'm telling you, I know that young woman. Perhaps she

favors your daughter, but her name is Cami Benrey." He groaned when it hit him. *Cami? Short for Camille?* "Oh m'goodness, Get in the car, Jackie, and I'll run inside and make our apologies."

The whispers stopped when Bubba rushed down the aisle to the front. "Sorry, folks. The wedding has been postponed. I wish I had time to explain, but it's an emergency. Thank you all for coming, and please feel free to go to the Reception Hall and enjoy the food."

As he ran out, he heard the preacher say, "Shall we pray?"

CHAPTER 31

Bubba ran to his car where Jackie was waiting. She leaned over the seat, opened his door and screamed, "What took you so long?"

"Calm down, hon. We'll find her. Did you see which way she went?"

Jackie pointed to a dirt road back of the church. "I don't get it, Bubba. She was on a motorcycle. Camille was always afraid of motorcycles. Hated them. It's now beginning to make sense why I never heard from her."

"Makes sense? Really? Clue me in, please. I have no idea what's going on."

"Don't you get it? My daughter has amnesia."

Bubba drove down the road, scattering dust behind the car, which had a dozen old shoes tied to the back and Just Married written on the back window.

He shook his head. "Cami? Amnesia? No way."

"What has she told you, Bubba. About her family, I mean."

He lifted a shoulder. "It's true she never told me about her childhood, but she has no problem recalling her marriage to Ian."

"That proves my point. She's confused. Camille isn't married."

"Jackie, Cami Benrey is a widow, and I know for a fact she was married to a very popular singer named Ian Benrey. She came here to work at the hospital with Dr. Carlos Cunningham."

"Oh, Bubba. She's a nurse? Really? Bless her heart. She's talked about being a nurse since she was a little girl, but Jacob would not hear to it. He insisted she pursue law. Hard to believe she's been living under my nose for months and I never ran into her." Jackie chewed on her thumbnail. "I know I'm rambling, but I'm nervous. She's slipped out of my life again. I have to find her."

"I promise we'll find her and you'll get answers to all your questions."

"Thank you, Bubba, but please go faster."

"Try to stay calm, sweetheart. I'm going as fast as I can on these roads."

Jackie pulled a couple of pins from her hat and tossed it over her shoulder to the back seat. "I'm so angry at myself for not questioning Lexi when she told me she was moving in with a girl named Cami from Tennessee. I should've picked up on it. I even called my daughter Cami when she was young. Oh, Bubba, why didn't I ask questions? Why?"

"Why would you? Lexi's roommate was Cami Benrey. Not

Camille Gorham. Camille disappeared from Virginia. Cami moved here from Tennessee. It's understandable that you wouldn't have put it together."

"But she came to my wedding, Bubba. Why would she come to my wedding and then bolt out the door before it began?"

"Sweetheart, she came to *my* wedding, not knowing it was also yours. Cami told me she looked forward to meeting my Jewel. It didn't register at the time, but I now suspect she misunderstood when I called you a jewel. She apparently assumed it to be your name."

After searching all the likely places for a pink and black Harley, Bubba took the nearest exit and turned the car around.

"What are you doing? Why are we turning back, for crying out loud?"

"You want the truth, Jackie? I'm at a loss. I have no clue where to look. If you have any ideas, please share them and I'll be happy to go in that direction. I have a feeling she's on the open road, riding until she gets her thoughts together, so I'm headed for I-10 unless you have a better suggestion."

"I'm sorry, darling, to have questioned your motivation. It's just—"

"No apology necessary. I want to find her, too, and I'm frustrated that I don't know which direction to take. Honey, I've never asked you, but I think it's something we might need to discuss. Did you and Cami have an argument before she left home? Some reason she wouldn't want to see you?"

"No. Everything was fine between us. It was better than fine, Bubba. We were very close. We shared everything."

"Everything?"

"Yes. You sound as if you doubt me." She slid over and hugged the door. "I have no reason to lie."

Bubba squeezed the steering wheel until his knuckles turned white. "It's understandable that our nerves are on edge, but there's no reason to snap at one another. I didn't say I doubted you, Jackie. I was curious to know if she was aware of how her birth came about. But if you shared *everything*—"

Jackie buried her face in her hands. "Everything but that."

Bubba's eyes squinted as he focused on the open road. There were pieces to this puzzle that didn't fit. Did he dare go there while Jackie was so distraught? He reached across the seat for her hand. "Sweetheart, you told me Wednesday that your daughter was dead. I didn't ask how you found out, but now I'm curious why you would've said that, since you're saying Cami is your daughter. Who told you she was dead?"

"The truth is, Bubba, people have been trying to convince me she was dead from the first day she went missing, but I refused to believe it. Wednesday, I decided I'd been fooling myself, and it was time to admit she was never coming back. But I was wrong. And they were wrong. My beautiful baby is alive and I won't stop until I find her. I can't lose her again. I can't!"

He reached in his shirt pocket, pulled out his cell phone and handed it to her. "Find Tucker in my contacts and call him."

"Tucker?"

"Yes. The guy she came to the wedding with."

"But she left alone."

"Please. Call him."

When Tucker answered, Jackie handed the phone to Bubba. "Yeah, Tuck, it's me. No. We haven't found her, and I've looked everywhere I know to look. It's a long story. I thought she might've gotten in touch with you, or that you could possibly give us insight in where she might've gone."

"Not a clue." Then immediately, he followed with, "Wait! It's a longshot, but worth a try. I didn't have my car at the church, so I rode back to the hospital with Carlos. Come pick me up. I have an idea."

"We're on I-10 at the Michigan Avenue Exit. Will be there shortly. Wait our front."

"Come around to the ER entrance."

Jackie whined. "If he knew where to look, why didn't he tell you, so we could be on our way instead of wasting time by going to the hospital?"

"Trust me, we would've wasted more time arguing. When Tucker McDowell makes up his mind, it's not easily changed. At least he seems to have an idea where we might look."

Bubba pulled up in front of the ER, and Tucker jumped in the back seat. "Let's go to Fairhope."

"Fairhope? Seriously? Why would you think she'd be there?"

"Her biker friends said they planned to meet a motorcycle club there after the wedding and would ride together to the Mayo Clinic in Jacksonville. Cami said if she didn't love her job, she'd be riding with them."

Whether intentional or not, Jackie's response sounded curt. "I know you mean well, young man, but that doesn't sound like my daughter."

Bubba glanced in the rear-view mirror and sensed Tucker's frustration.

Tucker snipped, "If you know where she is, then why don't you either tell us or keep quiet, because this is not a game of hide-and-seek we're playing. I love her and I'm willing to explore every angle until she's found."

Bubba threw up his hand. "Take it easy, Tucker. This is Cami's mother and she wants to find her as much as you do."

"Her *mother?* So, you're the reason she ran away?"

Bubba gave Tucker a sideways glance. "That's enough. Frankly, I agree with Jackie that riding with a crew of bikers to Jacksonville sounds unlikely. Cami wouldn't leave town. She's very responsible and loves her job at the hospital."

Jackie said, "I think we should go to her apartment and wait there for her to show up. She's obviously confused, so we'll all sit down, talk, and get this whole misunderstanding straightened out."

Tucker yelled, "Stop!"

Bubba glanced behind him and slammed on brakes. "What's wrong?"

"There they are—the bikers—parked at the gas station."

"Are you sure it's the same guys?"

"It's them, Bubba, but I don't see her bike."

Bubba's gaze met Jackie's. "I didn't expect to see it, Tucker. We've wasted enough time. We're going to the apartment."

Tucker said, "Let me out. Now!"

"Tuck, I don't think you really want to get out here. Cami obviously isn't with them."

"Do I have to jump out, or are you gonna stop the car?"

Bubba pressed the brakes, but Tucker was opening the door before the car came to a full stop.

"Thanks, Bubba."

"Sure, kid. We'll call you when we find her."

Tuck gave a salute. "Yeah. And I'll call you when I find her." He jogged back toward the station.

Bubba drove away, and Jackie said, "I feel bad leaving that young man with no way to get home, but frankly I'm glad you didn't waste time on that crazy hunch of his. Camille riding across state with a bunch of bikers? Ridiculous."

Bubba tapped his finger against the steering wheel. "Don't you worry about Tucker, hon. He'll have no problem getting someone to take him home. But I'll assure you, you won't find better people than Cross-T and the guys. I've known them for eons. But the notion of Cami leaving a great job and riding off with men she barely knows, doesn't jive. However, I'm learning there's a lot about her that I don't know, and there's the possibility she may not be the same girl you knew several years ago."

It was evident from Jackie's puckered lips that his comment wasn't well received. "She's my daughter, Bubba. No one knows her better than I. Whenever she was blue, she always wanted to be alone. Mark my word, when we find her, she'll be in a solitary place, not carousing around with strange men. The year she was a freshman in high school, she tried out for cheerleader and lost. For two days, she stayed in her room and refused to come out." Jackie smiled, though her eyes revealed her pain. "She worked so hard the next year, determined to win. And not only did she win, but she became Head Cheerleader. That girl of mine is no quitter. If something bothers her, she gets alone until she figures out a way to overcome the problem."

"Honey, we'll go to the garage apartment and I have a hunch from what you've told me about her, that she'll either call Lexie or show up there. She has nowhere else to go. But we'll find her. I promise you we'll find her. I love her, too."

CHAPTER 32

Lexie ran out to meet Bubba's car and searched the back seat with her eyes. Her shoulders slumped. Bubba watched the air seep from her lips. Her voice trembled. "No?"

He shook his head. "No, Lex. Couldn't find her. We were hoping she was here."

"Oh, Bubba, I can't understand it. I've been watching out the window, since Jamal dropped me off. When I saw you drive up, I was positive Cami would be in the car with you."

They walked into the apartment and Lexie threw her arms around Jackie. "I am so sorry, Mama J. She's my best friend, but I feel like strangling her for ruining your wedding. I have no idea what caused her to go berserk like that."

"Oh, honey, I don't know either, but she didn't ruin my wedding. This is the happiest day of my life. My daughter's alive."

"Your *daughter*? Really? That's awesome, Jackie. I know how you've wanted to believe she was alive. Where is she? Was she at the wedding?"

"What do you mean, was she at the wedding?"

Bubba said, "Lexie, it's Cami. Cami is Jackie's daughter."

Jackie nodded. "Oh, I'm sorry. I wasn't thinking. You had no way of knowing."

Lexie's jaw dropped. "Oh my word. Cami—and your Camille—?" She popped her palm to her forehead. "No way." Her eyes squinted. "That's impossible. You must be mistaken, Jackie."

"No, honey. I saw her. Remember? I know my own daughter."

"But how can that be? Cami couldn't have been referring to you when she said she lost her mother."

Jackie burst into tears. "She told you I was dead?"

Lexi lifted a shoulder. "I never thought she meant literally—I figured she meant dead to her."

Jackie said, "Oh, Bubba, what did I tell you? Camille has amnesia. That's the only explanation why she doesn't remember me and couldn't find her way home."

Lexie shook her head. "I don't want to burst your bubble, Jackie, but I'm confident we can't be talking about the same person. You said your daughter has been gone for several years. People change. It's possible Cami and Camille not only share the same name, but they obviously favor."

Jackie shook her head. "No, Lexie. I saw her. She's my baby, and I need to find her and tell her how much I love her—how I've missed her every hour of every day since she's been gone."

Bubba said, "Honey, if your theory is right and the reason she couldn't find her way home or remember you is because she suffers from amnesia, then would it make sense that she'd run away when she sees you?"

Jackie threw up her hands. "I don't know. I don't know anything, anymore. The only thing I can be sure of is that my daughter is alive. I don't know much about amnesia, but perhaps when she couldn't remember me, she assumed her mother was dead—yet, when she saw me today, something triggered a memory and poor little thing was frightened because she couldn't put the jumbled pieces together." Her eyes widened.

Bubba said, "What's wrong?"

"I know what frightened her."

"You do?"

"Yes. Why was I so stupid not to think of it earlier? I think her memory returned when she saw me. But seeing me, as a bride, walking down the aisle must have been a terrible shock to her. Don't you get it, Bubba? She didn't know about her father's death. He was never the doting father I'd hoped he'd be, but still, he was her daddy, and it must've been traumatizing for her to see me marrying another man. She had to wonder what happened to her daddy."

Lexie said, "Hold on. That proves we aren't talking about the same person. Cami wasn't fond of either of her parents."

"No. That's not true. Camille and I were very close."

"Jackie, trust me, Cami would've loved to have had a mother like you. But she had no respect for her mom. From what she told me, her mother was involved in numerous adulterous affairs, and the man she married was not Cami's father, although Cami didn't learn the truth until the day she left home."

Jackie's eyes squinted. "That doesn't make sense. The girl you call Cami who ran out of the church is your roommate. Right?"

"Right."

"Well, I saw her. And your roommate is definitely my daughter, but none of those things you claim she told you are correct."

Lexie bristled. "I have no reason to lie."

"Oh, honey, I'm sorry, if it sounded as if I were accusing you. I'm only trying to sort things out."

Bubba said, "I think we're all a little on edge and rightfully so. Lexie, try to remember . . . is there's anything else Cami might've told you about her past that might give us all a clue to what's going on with her?"

"She talked about her husband. A *lot!*"

He said, "Actually, I'm more interested in knowing what she said about her childhood. You mentioned she wasn't particularly fond of her parents. What else did she say about her relationship with her mom and dad?"

Jackie said, "It's the amnesia, Bubba. We had a wonderful relationship. Not only mother and daughter, but we were best friends."

Bubba said, "Honey, let's listen and let Lexie try to recall anything that might give us a clue to this mystery. Be prepared, though. You may hear things you don't want to hear."

Lexie nodded. "I'm trying to think of something, which might help put the pieces together, yet, we mostly talked about—" She snapped her fingers. "Wait! I do remember something. She claimed her Mom lied to both her and to the man Cami grew up believing to be her father."

Jackie interrupted. "See? It's the amnesia. She's confused. I'll wager there's never been a mother and daughter closer, and Camille would have no reason to question that Jacob Gorham was her father."

Bubba placed his hand on her arm. "I know this is hard, honey, but please let Lexie finish."

Lexie lowered her gaze, as if she couldn't face either of them. "I feel I'm being disloyal to Cami by repeating our private conversations. Why don't we wait until she comes back and let her explain?"

Bubba said, "I know it isn't easy for you, Lex, but we can't be sure that she will return. It's important that we know what she's thinking, so we can help find her if we can."

She nodded. "I suppose you're right, but I wish there was some other way. Jackie, I love you, and I don't want to say anything else that could cause you more pain."

Bubba locked his hands back of his head and leaned back. "I know you don't want to hurt Jackie, Lex, and neither do I. But anything you can remember could be very important and could possibly lead to Jackie getting her daughter back. So, please, tell us anything you remember that might be a link to her past."

Lexie glanced at Jackie, then lowered her gaze. "Cami said her mother tricked a man into marrying her, because she was pregnant with another man's baby. Cami told me she was the baby. She claimed the man she called daddy was not a very nice man, but she actually felt sorry for him and understood why he never felt close to her, since he was tricked into the marriage. She said her mother had always pretended to be so virtuous. But the man she thought was her father was drunk one day and spilled the beans. He told her he knew she wasn't his daughter from the day she was born. Claimed he'd suspected all along, but when she was born, she had red hair, and apparently Cami's mother's lover was a redhead."

Bubba felt heat rising from his neck to the top of his head. "Jackie, are you thinking what I'm thinking?"

"Yes. Oh, Bubba, Jacob was a cruel man, but this was even low down for him. He convinced her that I was—" She pressed her fist against her mouth. "No wonder she left home. Bubba, we have to find her and tell her the truth."

Lexie said, "Wait. It's you, isn't it Bubba? Red hair. You're Cami's father? Wow. No wonder she took off when she saw the two of you together."

"No, Lexie, I'm *not* her father. True, I was in love with Jackie before Cami was born and we'd hoped to one day get married, although we were too young at the time. But Jackie was raped by Jacob Gorham and when her parents discovered she was pregnant, they forced him to marry her."

Lexie said, "So you never told her that Jacob raped you?"

Her lip trembled. "Of course not. How could I? I was afraid of what it would do to her if she grew up believing her father was a rapist. I couldn't do that to her."

Bubba said, "I understand why you didn't tell her, Jackie , but you have no choice, now. She has to know the truth."

"No. I won't and neither of you should say anything, either. It would be cruel to tell her."

"Cruel to whom? To Jacob? You're choosing to protect *him?*"

"Of course not. But don't you see? She'll feel she carries the genes of a reprobate."

"That would be the truth, Jackie, but it doesn't mean she's a reprobate."

"No. I've kept it from her all these years. She's not to ever know the truth."

Bubba's jaw shot out. "So you'd rather her think you're a . . . a woman with no morals who slept with me before you were married? I'm sorry, Jackie, but if it's more important to you to protect Jacob Gorham's memory than to protect my reputation, then maybe Cami saved us from making a big mistake."

"You're not being rational, Bubba."

"Irrational, am I? Well, why don't you stay here and wait, and I'll go home and let you deal with the situation with whatever feel-good fairytales you wish to concoct, but I want no part of it."

Jackie grabbed his arm. "We're both upset, darling, and saying things we don't mean. It's been a very stressful day. Please, wait with me."

Bubba looked down at her hand grasping his arm. "Turn loose, Jackie."

Lexie said, "Please don't go, Bubba. I should've kept my mouth shut. This is all my fault."

He shook his head. "No. You told the truth. You aren't the one who has chosen to perpetuate the lies."

"A liar? That's what you think I am?" Jackie drew back and crossed her arms over her chest.

Bubba reached in his pocket for his keys. "I'm done."

CHAPTER 33

Bubba drove up to the small bungalow he'd called home for over twenty years. It wasn't until he opened the door that he realized he hadn't planned on coming back there after the wedding, and had taken all his clothes to Jackie's place.

He went to the laundry room, hoping to find something left behind he could change into. He saw a cardboard box, which he'd intended to take to Goodwill, dug through it until he found a pair of shorts and a tee shirt. For hours, he'd imagined how great it would feel to get out of the suit and tie and get into something more comfortable.

Strange, it didn't feel as good as he'd hoped. He pulled back the covers on the bed and lay down. *My wedding night.* After tossing and turning for almost an hour, he jumped up, grabbed his keys from the bedside table and headed out the door, on his way to Cami's. Was it too much to expect Jackie to forgive him? His eyes clouded with tears as he drove past the cottage on 104 Bay Street that he'd planned to share with his wife. Wife? If she never spoke to him again, he couldn't blame her. What caused him to say such hateful things? It was so unlike him. He'd never had a temper problem, yet the hot, vile words spewed from his mouth as if flowing from an uncapped well.

He pulled up in front of the garage apartment, but didn't ring the doorbell. Instead, he beat on the door with his fist. "Jackie, it's me. Please, please let me in." His heart sank when a light came on, but no one came to the door. "I beg you, honey. Please, let me in. I was so wrong. I love you, Jackie. I always have and I always will."

The door opened and Jackie threw her arms around his neck.

Bubba's voice broke. "Thank you. I was afraid you weren't going to open the door and I wouldn't have blamed you."

"Silly man, I was so excited when I heard your voice. I couldn't wait to see you, but I had dressed for bed and was trying to find something presentable."

"You aren't only presentable, but you're the most beautiful thing I've ever seen. Jackie, I don't know what got into me, tonight, to make me say—"

"Shh! You'll wake Lexie." She pressed her lips to his, and no further explanations were needed.

Jackie said, "Would you drink a cup of coffee if I made a pot?"

"I'd love a cup of coffee."

"Bubba, I've thought about what you said, and you're right.

When we find her, I promise to tell her the truth."

"Jackie, you do what you feel in your heart is right. Don't listen to me. What do I know? I've never had a child."

****

Cross-Tee said, "So, Tucker, you're telling us you really believe she'll be at the Pier?"

"I'll bet on it."

"But from what she told us, she has the dream job. You really think she'd run off and leave it?"

"I do. According to Bubba's niece, Keely, it's not the first time she's run away."

"Are you talking about when she made the trip from Tennessee to Alabama, because I don't think she was running away. She left in hopes of landing the hospital job."

"No, I'm talking about when she left home, back before she met her husband. I don't know everything that went on, or why she left, but I gathered from Keely that Cami left home angry with her parents. Keely said all Cami would say, was that they lied, and she never wanted to see them again. So, to answer your question, 'yes, I think it's very likely that she'd run off and leave a good job.
I've sensed that Cami has something boiling inside her and the only way she knows to escape is to distance herself from it. I understand."

Cross-Tee said, "So would you like for me to call you if we get to the Pier and she's there?"

"No, I want to go with you."

"But how would you get back, if she isn't there?"

"No sweat. I have a condo near the pier. I'll sleep there tonight and call someone to come get me tomorrow."

As they approached the beach, Tucker yelled, "I see her bike."

As soon as Cross-Tee parked, the other bikers pulled up in a row beside them, and Tucker jumped off and ran, calling her name.

"There she is," one of the guys yelled.

Tucker turned and looked in the direction, then ran toward her. "Hey, you left me at the church. I rode there with you, remember? Why did you leave me?"

Her eyes squinted. "What are you doing here, Tucker, and how did you know where to find me?"

"I have my ways." He hopped on the back of her bike. "Come on, let's go to Mobile."

"Get off, Tucker. I didn't tell you to come looking for me. You'll have to find another way back. I'm leaving."

Cross-Tee stepped away from his bike. "I don't think that's a wise idea, Li'l Darling. You're a sweetheart, but I've come to realize you have a bad habit that has become a serious problem. And knowing Chap as we did, I'm sure he wouldn't want us to become enablers. He'd expect us to leave you and let you work it out. I'm sure of it. It's for your own good."

"So you aren't gonna let me ride with you?"

"Wish we could, Li'l Darling, but out of respect for the Chap, it just wouldn't be right."

She threw up her hands. "That's crazy. I have no idea what

you're talking about. You don't even know me that well. Please, Cross-Tee? Please, get me away from here. I can't stay."

He glanced over his shoulder at the bikers waiting for the go-ahead. "Gotta run, Li'l Darling."

"Wait! What bad habit were you referring to? You can't go without at least telling me why you won't take me?"

"Fair enough. Cami, you have a bad habit of running from your fears. It's time to plant your feet on the ground, stand firm, and face life with all its uncertainties."

"Running away . . . So you think that's what I'm doing?"

"Isn't it?"

She wanted to object, but the words wouldn't come. They wouldn't come because Cross-Tee was right. But how would he know? Her chin quivered as she nodded in affirmation. "You guys will keep in touch?"

"You bet!"

She glanced over at Tucker, waiting on the back of her bike, as if he'd known all along that she'd be heading back to Mobile.

Cross-Tee said, "Give me a hug before you go." He threw up his hand as he cranked his bike. "I'll expect you two to send me an invitation when you set a date."

Cami's mouth flew open. "A date? Surely, you jest. Not gonna happen in a million years."

Tucker grinned. "Pshhh! Be checking your mail, Cross-Tee."

Cami whirled around and faced Tucker. What was it about this guy that drew her to him? Was it pity for a young man, dying in his prime? No, It wasn't pity. Compassion? She couldn't verbalize it, but one thing for sure—it went much deeper than compassion. She had compassion for her patients but never had she had a single one who could literally take her breath away. Her gaze locked with his and a smile sneaked across her lips. *What kind of hold do you have on me, Tucker McDowell?* The handsome hunk glaring back at her had no tact, could be unquestionably rude, and though he was all man, she was sometimes shocked by his off-the-wall, childlike responses. Still, there was no denying, she was drawn to him.

He returned her smile and a crazy electric flush ran through her body. Cami's knees turned to jelly. She'd only felt this strange phenomenon one time in her life—the first day she crawled on the back of Ian Benrey's bike, with no idea where life was taking her. For some crazy reason, it didn't seem to matter. She'd taken a risk, yet she'd never felt as safe. Like she was exactly where she needed to be. She remembered it well.

As she rode away, she felt Tucker's arms wrap around her waist.

Her heart hammered.

Déjà vu.

CHAPTER 34

Cross-Tee said Ian would want her to face her fears. He apparently knew her husband well, for she couldn't deny it was exactly the advice Ian would've given her, and as always, her wise husband would've been right.

Well, she could do this. And she would. But if she was lucky, she'd have a week before her mother and Bubba returned from their honeymoon. Her imagination worked overtime, conjuring up make-believe scenarios—some good, most bad, as she rehearsed what she'd say to her mother, when once again, they'd come face-to-face.

Chills ran down her spine. To think of all the evenings that she'd sat and chatted with Bubba at the diner, waiting for Lexie to get off work, and not once did he even hint that he was her biological father. The man was as big a liar as her mother, and a leech, no doubt, to allow another man to foot the bills that should've belonged to him.

No wonder Jacob Gorham resented her. They hardly ever talked and when they did, she was asking for money. All her life, she'd longed for a daddy's love, and now she understood why Jacob was unable to give her what she craved. He wasn't her daddy. Cami recalled their last conversation, the day she ran away. Well, no more running. She'd face her mother and Bubba, have her say, and after that she'd have no reason to be around either of them.

The return trip from Fairhope back to Mobile seemed much longer than the ride there. Come to think of it, she could barely remember getting there. Her mind had been on all the lies fed to her from her childhood. How could she have been so wrong about her mother? The tears felt warm against her face.

She rode up to her apartment and parked her bike beside Tucker's car. He hopped off first, then held out his hand for hers. The strain of the emotional day hit her like a category five hurricane—it had been slow to come, but when it landed, it hit with a devastating force. "Hold me, Tuck. Hold me tight." She collapsed in his arms, with her head resting against his broad chest.

"Hey, are you crying? Please don't cry." He gently kissed her forehead, then touched his cheek to hers. Her pulse raced when she felt their tears mingle.

"Cami, I'm crying!" He repeated it, adding emphasis. "I'm

crying! Really crying." He raised his head and pointed. "Look. These are *my* tears. Well, some are yours, but mostly mine."

She'd never seen anyone so happy to be shedding tears.

"All my life, I've heard, 'You have no compassion, Tucker. No compassion.' Made me feel like a freak. I didn't even know how to fake it. But if I understand correctly, compassion is hurting when someone else is hurting. Is that right?"

"Your definition is close enough, Tucker." She reached up and wiped his cheek. What a precious soul. Childlike, for sure, but she wouldn't swap him for any other man on the planet.

"Well, I've got it. I'm compassionate. It happened before I knew it was coming. When I saw your tears, I felt this peculiar pain in my chest and the next thing I knew, my eyes were watering, and my lip was quivering. That's compassion isn't it?"

She laughed, though tears streamed down her cheeks. "Yes, indeed, and I love your new-found compassion."

"You're still crying but you're laughing at the same time. I don't think I can do that."

"It's a girl thing. It means everything is gonna be okay. It's been a long day, and I'm quite tired." She reached up and pecked him on the lips. "Goodnight, Tucker. Be careful driving home."

"I want to walk you to the door."

Cami stuck her key in the keyhole, but before she could turn the knob, the door swung open.

She let out a loud groan, when her mother grabbed her in her arms, hugging her tightly. Cami stood rigid, refusing to respond to the unwarranted show of affection. The bitter taste of bile rose to her throat when she saw Bubba standing behind her mother. How could she have been so wrong about them both?

Cami reached for Tucker's hand. "You might as well come in and join the party. It looks like we were the last to be invited." She stomped over to the sofa and patted the seat beside her for Tucker. If her eyes could've shot arrows, her mother would have been severely wounded. In a sharp tone, she barely recognized as belonging to her, she said, "What are you two doing here?"

Jackie said, "You have no idea how much I've missed you, sweetheart. We need to talk. Bubba and I have been waiting for you to get here."

"You have nothing to say to me that I don't already know, so you've wasted time by waiting up. I figured you'd be off on a long-awaited honeymoon, laughing at how you fooled me into thinking Jacob was my father. Well, you may have fooled me once, but you won't fool me twice, so whatever you came here to say, can be left unsaid."

Jackie's body shook as she sobbed. "Camille, Honey, I know you're angry, but I never lied to you."

"Really, Mom? Never? And what about your husband? You plan to tell me with a straight face that you didn't lie to him, either? Well, let me tell you a secret, Mommy dearest . . . he knew. Jacob said he'd known from the first day he saw me in the hospital nursery. He wrote me off his expense account the day I left home. I'm guessing he finally got smart and took you off, also."

Bubba said, "Cami, all that your mother and I ask, is that you sit down and let us tell you the truth."

Cami said, "After twenty-four years of living a lie, are you really sure you know how to tell the truth, Bubba?" She smirked. "Or should I call you, *father?*"

"No, because I'm not your father?"

"Well, better luck with number three, Mom. You've now had two men who vehemently deny they fathered your baby. I wonder who my daddy is, don't you?"

Jackie's body shook with sobs.

"Look on the bright side, Mom. You and I could go on that disgusting TV Show, with a plea for all possible candidates to please come forward and take a DNA test. We might snag one with even more money than the Gorham family."

Bubba said, "Cami, you're angry, and I get it. But you have no idea what you're talking about. You might want to stretch out and get comfortable while I tell you the truth, because this may take a while."

She picked up a throw pillow from the sofa and tossed it in Tucker's lap, then stretched out with her head resting on the pillow. "Fine. I'm comfy. Start talking, but I have a feeling we should have a violinist to get the full effect of your sordid love story." Tucker reached down and caressed her cheek with his hand but said nothing.

Bubba's Adam's apple bobbed. "Before we begin, why don't you let us know the questions that you have, so we can separate fact from fiction?"

"Gladly. First of all, why did Uncle Johnny agree to give you away, Mom, after the cruel trick you played on his brother?"

Cami's pulse raced as she listened to Bubba and her mother pour out a long, shocking story that spanned over two-decades. It was not the story she expected to hear. Her voice quivered. "So, Jacob really *was* my father?"

"Yes, honey, but Jacob's mother—your grandmother—resented me because my parents forced their son to marry me. My family was not in the same league with the prestigious Gorhams."

"But that's crazy that your parents would want you to marry a man who raped you."

"Yes, it was. I didn't love him. But Jacob's father was an important political figure. To prevent my parents from causing a scandal that could ruin his career, the Gorhams were forced to comply, and we were whisked off to Virginia, where you were born six months later."

"Then Jacob lied to me when he told me he wasn't my father?"

"It was a lie, but I think he convinced himself it was true, after his mother brought up the red hair. Honey, I am so sorry you had to learn the truth about how your birth came about, but I loved you from the moment you were born. I couldn't have loved you more if you'd been conceived out of a loving relationship. I'm so sorry. I never wanted you to know."

Cami sat up. "Tucker, thank you for everything. It's late, and I know you're tired. Call me tomorrow?"

"Yeah. Are you sure you're okay?"

"I'm fine. Goodnight."

She walked him to the door, then ambled back and plopped down on the sofa. "Oh, Mom, Cross-Tee was right."

"Cross Tee? I don't understand."

She smiled through the tears and shook her head. "Cross-Tee, a biker friend, told me I had a bad habit of running away from my fears. That's exactly what I did the day Jacob Gorham told me he wasn't my father. I thought everything I'd always believed about you was a lie and instead of facing you to allow you an opportunity to explain, I bolted. I couldn't face the truth."

Bubba glanced at his watch. "So does this mean it's all good?"

Cami hugged her Mom. "Not *all*. I'm so ashamed that I ruined your wedding. I feel awful and don't know how I'll ever face the people in this town. Bubba, I'm sorry I misjudged you. Would you like to know the truth?"

He gave a little chuckle. "I prefer it."

"I wish you were my father. I mean it. You would've made a great daddy."

His eyes glistened. "Thank you, Cami. I wish it, too. You have no idea how much I wish I were your dad."

CHAPTER 35

Jackie said, "Camille, honey, Bubba told me that you're a widow. I'm so sorry, sweetheart. I wish I could've met him. I understand he was a famous entertainer?"

"Oh, Mom, I wish you could've met him, too. Everyone who knew Ian, loved him, but no one could've loved him as much as I did. He was wonderful."

"It breaks my heart that you've had to endure so much heartache."

"But don't you see? If I'd never left home when I did, I wouldn't have met Ian, so therefore, there's only one thing I would change if I could. I'll never forgive myself for stopping your wedding."

Bubba said, "Cami, please don't worry, because you haven't stopped the wedding. It was simply delayed."

247

Jackie smiled. "He's right."

Cami's cell rang. She pulled it from her pocket. "Excuse me. It's Tucker." She put it on speakerphone.

He said, "Cami, how's it going there?"

"It's all good, Tucker."

"I didn't know if I should've left you when I did."

"That was very thoughtful of you to call."

"Really?"

She smiled. "Yes, really. Mom, Bubba and I talked everything out. It's amazing how things got so wound around because of all the twisted truths and downright lies."

"Twisted truth and downright lies are both the same thing, Cami."

She tried not to laugh. "I stand corrected."

"Cami, if you love someone and plan to marry them, you won't keep secrets. Even if there are things you don't want them to know about you, you'll tell them. Right?"

Her throat tightened. She'd wanted him to open up about his tumor, but why would he choose now? This wasn't something she wished to discuss with an audience.

"Tucker, could we please talk tomorrow?"

"Sure. But Cami, I need to tell you something you don't know. I have Asperger's. There. I said it."

There was a long silence.

"Cami, are you angry?"

"No. Of course not." She looked at her mom and Bubba who

sat quietly. He seemed fine earlier, but now, he wasn't making sense. Had she placed him under undue stress? "Uh . . . yes, Tucker, I'm familiar with Asperger's."

She mouthed an apology to Bubba and her mom for staying on the phone so long. "Tucker, what made you think of Asperger's?"

"I don't know. Forget it. Want to meet me for lunch tomorrow at the hospital cafeteria?"

"Tucker, I think I know what you wanted to tell me."

"You do?"

"It was about the brain tumor. Am I right?" She sucked in a deep breath and waited.

"What brain tumor?"

"I overheard the phone conversation with you and your doctor. I wish there was something I could do to help."

"My doctor has a brain tumor?"

"Not your doctor. You can talk to me."

"Sheesh, Cami, you should understand why a Radiologist wouldn't be able to discuss someone's medical condition, even if I had a clue who the patient is you're referring to. Can we talk about something else?"

She placed her hand over the phone and whispered to Bubba and Jackie. "Excuse me. I had no idea it would take this long. You've probably noticed he sometimes acts a bit bizarre."

Bubba grinned. "Just a bit."

"He's sick, Bubba. Tucker has a brain tumor and has begun to hallucinate. Bless his heart, he just told me he's a Radiologist."

Bubba's jaw dropped. "A brain tumor?"

Cami could hold the tears back no longer. Not wanting Tucker to hear her sobbing, she blurted over the phone. "Sorry, Tuck. Something's come up. I need to go."

"Hold on. Cami, since it appears to be common knowledge, I'm interested in knowing which of my doctors has a brain tumor. Is it Dr. Jennings? He does act a little off-the-wall, sometimes."

"Tucker, it's not the doctor. You've been in and out of the hospital a lot lately. Right?"

"Yep."

"Do you remember why?"

"Because I work there?"

"No. You go there because—" She held the phone away from her ear when he blurted, "Oh, no. No! It can't be true."

Cami pounded her fist to her forehead. Why didn't she leave well enough alone? Was it so important that he face the truth? After a long, awkward silence, she said, "Tucker, are you okay?"

"No, I'm not okay. Oh, babe. I wish we could switch places."

"What?"

"You've been trying to tell me. It's not the doctor. I get it, now. You're the one with the brain tumor. The signs were there, and I should've picked up on them. All this time, I thought it was autism."

"Autism? *Me?* No, not me. I'm fine."

"You are?" Tucker blew out a puff of air. "Geez, I feel like I'm on a Carousel, spinning around and around."

Her heart hammered. "Do you need me to come over? Who's your doctor?"

Tucker let out a groan. "You mean the one who has the brain tumor?"

"Oh, Tuck, forget the doctor with the brain tumor. He doesn't exist."

"Wait a minute. So, you're saying the doctor doesn't have a tumor, I don't have a tumor and you claim not to have one. So, how did we get on the subject of non-existent brain tumors?"

"It's not non-existent. I heard the whole phone conversation . . . at least from your end, when you were discussing it with your doctor."

Tucker said, "Really? Please. Refresh my memory."

Her lips pressed together into a straight line. Did she dare? Perhaps she should play along, pretend he was well and that she simply misunderstood?

"I'm waiting."

Cami learned in school that it was always best to be upfront with a patient, truthfully answering all their questions. She sucked in a lungful of air, then slowly exhaled. "Tucker, you repeated his diagnosis. Glioblastoma. You asked the doctor how much longer you'd have, and I sensed you were stunned at the answer you received." She stopped. "Are you all right? Shall I continue?"

"Yes, please do. If I'm dying, I'd like to know my expiration date."

Was he being facetious or truly attempting to remember

details, which were slowly escaping? "You said two weeks wasn't much time to get your things in order, but you'd be ready to go when your time comes."

"But, Tucker, we've already surpassed that time limit. Doctors don't know everything. There's no way of really knowing, and we'll make the best of the time we have left."

When he chuckled, Cami's heart sank. Was he in denial? "I'm so sorry, Tucker. I wish there was something I could do."

"I accept your apology, but do you make a habit of listening in on other people's private phone conversations? Sheesh, I'm told my social skills are lacking, but even I know that's not nice."

She bit her tongue. "I was sitting directly across from you when you received the call. It's not as if I purposely eavesdropped." Was she allowing herself to become angry with Tucker, when clearly, the tumor was growing and he had no memory of the conversation? She was a nurse, for goodness sake. And until she met Tucker McDowell, she had considered herself to be a very good one. Now, she wasn't so sure.

CHAPTER 36

Tucker said, "We're talking in circles. Hang up the phone, Cami. I'm coming over. We need to talk face-to-face until we get things straight. Seems there are things you don't know about me and things you think you know."

"No, don't come. It's late, and—"

Realizing he'd hung up, she laid the phone on the mantle. "He's on his way over."

Ten minutes later, Tucker was knocking on the door. She let him in and walked him over to the sofa. "It wasn't necessary for you to come. It's late, and I have to work tomorrow."

"So do I."

Her heart wrenched.

He reached for her hand and clasped it firmly between his two palms. "Now, would you like to know the other half of that phone conversation?"

"It's not necessary, Tucker. I tried to tell you not to come. We don't have to talk about it."

"Well, I think we do. The call was from Dr. Sears, from Memphis. He asked if I'd speak on Glioblastoma at a Medical Conference. He apologized for the late notice, since I'd only have two weeks to make arrangements, but he'd had a last-minute cancellation. It didn't give me much time to fit it into my schedule, but he's always helped me whenever I've called on him, so I agreed."

Cami felt her face grow hot with embarrassment, when Bubba and her Mom bowed over with laughter. Bubba said, "I suppose I won't need to order that black suit. I was sure you'd want me to be one of your Pall Bearers."

Cami shot a sharp glance Bubba's way. "Not funny. I'm really sorry, Tucker. I don't know what else to say, except I've never been so thrilled to be wrong."

Tucker swiped his hand across his forehead. "And to think, I worried about telling you I had Asperger's. I had no idea you had me dying from a killer tumor."

She squealed and grabbed him around the neck. "Oh, Tucker. Asperger's? Are you serious? That's awesome." Her lip lifted at the corner. "But you *were* pulling my leg about being a Radiologist. Right? I mean, if you have Asperger's—"

"I'm on the spectrum Cami, but I'm not brain dead. I graduated at the top of my class. I suppose Carlos was right, and I should've told you earlier, but I was afraid I'd run you off. I have a habit of alienating people."

"But why did you tell me you were an art critic?"

"I didn't. You're the one who called me an art critic."

"When I asked you what you did for a living, did you not tell me that you studied pictures all day, leaving me to assume you were a critic?"

"True, I told you I study pictures. X-rays. I never hinted that I judged art. I'm often accused of being rude, but you jumped to a conclusion without allowing me to finish, so I left it alone."

She sighed. "I seem to have a bad habit of jumping to erroneous conclusions. But if you're a Radiologist, why does everyone call you Tucker?"

He rolled his eyes. "It's my name?"

"Seems they'd refer to you as Dr. McDowell. I've never heard anyone call you anything other than Tucker. I find that a bit peculiar."

He pursed his lips. "Do you, now? And how do you find *me*?"

A smile slowly crept across her face. "A bit peculiar?"

"I thought you'd catch on. My friends call me Tucker and as surprising as that might sound to you, I have lots of friends."

Lexie lumbered into the den, wearing a robe and rubbing her eyes. "What's going on? I heard laughter."

Cami said, "Sorry if we woke you."

"No problem. I wanted to wait up with Bubba and Jackie for you to come home, but I was tired and figured they wouldn't mind if I left them alone. I didn't hear you come in." She handed Cami an envelope. "This came in the mail for you yesterday, and I forgot to give it to you."

Cami ripped open the small manila envelope. After gawking at the contents for several minutes, she stuck it in her pocket. She'd completely put the settlement for Ian's wrongful death out of her mind. The check was for more money than she could ever make in a lifetime, but there wasn't enough cash in the world to make up for her husband's untimely demise. Her stomach felt as if she'd swallowed a pack of needles. It didn't feel right to benefit from his death. What would she do with so much money? Her heart leaped when the answer came. Of course. Donate it to research for Autism Spectrum Disorder.

Jackie said, "Cami, honey, you look pale. Is it bad news?"

"No, Mom. Everything is gonna be fine."

Lexie said, "I heard laughter and thought I was missing something. I'm going back to bed." She turned to go back upstairs, then stopped. "Wait. I suppose now that everyone has kissed and made up, the wedding is back on? When's the date?"

Bubba and Jackie exchanged glances. "We haven't discussed it."

Lexie ambled back up the stairs. "Goodnight, all."

"The wedding!" Cami picked up the phone punched in a number.

Jackie said, "Honey, who are you calling at such a late hour?"

She placed her index finger over her lips, then said, "Keely, did I wake you?"

"Actually, you did. It's one o'clock. What do you want?"

"You sound angry."

"Do I? Are you surprised?"

"You *are* angry. I made a mistake, Keely. A whopper, and I want to make it up to Mom and Bubba."

"You spoiled what should've been the happiest day of their lives, Cami. How do you hope to make that up to them?"

"Keely, you worked hard on planning the wedding, and you have every right to hate me, but please listen to my idea."

"Fine, but make it quick. I'm tired."

"Have you taken down the decorations from the Family Life Center?"

"No, I was not in the mood, tonight. I'll do it tomorrow morning."

"I have a suggestion. Could you leave everything in place until Sunday?"

"I suppose so. Why?"

"Let's have a do-over after the church service."

"But I thought you . . ."

"I was wrong. Wrong about everything. The flowers should hold up a couple of days, don't you think?"

"Yes! I'm sorry for snapping at you, Cami. That's a great idea. There was lots food left over, and we stored it in the refrigerators at the church, thinking we'd come up with somewhere to send it tomorrow." She laughed. "I should say, today. It's already tomorrow. Since Bubba and Jackie left before the reception, we didn't have the heart to cut the wedding cake. Have Bubba and Jackie ready and we'll see that the knot gets properly tied this time."

CHAPTER 37

At the Sunday morning Worship Service, the Pastor said, "It's my privilege to announce that Bubba Knox and Mrs. Jackie Gorham will be reciting their marriage vows at the close of the service. They invite each of you to stay and offer your prayers as you witness this union. There's food in the Family Life Center, so, please, join the newly married couple for a reception, afterward."

Jackie appeared even more radiant than she had two nights before. Once again, her brother-in-law, Johnny Gorham, walked her down the aisle. Lexie bowed out as Jackie's bridesmaid, insisting that Cami take her place and wear the lavender organza dress. Trey was Bubba's Best Man and Tucker, a Groomsman, looked like a million bucks in his navy suit.

When the preacher asked, "Who gives this woman?" Johnny reached for Cami's hand and said, "Her daughter and I."

The happy couple ran out the door and Jackie tossed her bouquet behind her back. The crowd applauded when Cami caught it.

Tucker said, "Doesn't that mean you have to get married next?"

"*Have* to? Next? No. Certainly not."

"What does it mean?"

"It means I'm a better catcher than the others."

"Oh."

****

After the wedding, Cami helped Keely load her van with all the paraphernalia, then Keely took her home. Cami reached for her sweater and wrapped it around her shoulders. "Why don't you come in, toss off these heels and let's unwind with a glass of sweet iced tea."

"Aww, sounds awesome. You talked me into it."

Cami brought two tall glasses of iced tea and sat them on the drum table. "Keely, I haven't had a chance to tell you how sorry I was to hear about . . ." She stalled. "I'm sorry, I don't know what to call him. The man who raised you."

"Thanks. And I know what you mean, because I've never known what to call Wylie Gafford, either. Growing up, I sometimes called him Daddy, and other times I called him by his given name and he answered to both. I didn't think he had a preference, yet, he left me a letter before he died and signed it 'Daddy.' I can't explain, Cami, and I know no one can understand—but it warmed my heart."

"Why do you think no one would understand?"

"Those closest to me think I should hate him. After all, Wylie kidnapped me. Stole my childhood, broke my parents' hearts, and they spent thousands of dollars searching for me. He beat me with his belt so many times I lost count, leaving whelps on my body, but it was the verbal abuse that caused me the most pain."

"I understand the conflict."

"Do you? Because if you do, you're the only one who seems to understand. I wanted to hate him. I tried, but I couldn't. I couldn't any more than I could leave him when I was growing up and had the chance. I even stashed away a little money once, got on a bus to leave town—then stopped the bus before it got out of town. Couldn't leave him. Sounds crazy, I know."

"Not to me. You and I share a similar experience. Not that I was kidnapped, but I lived with a man I called 'Daddy,' yet he never loved me. He didn't physically abuse me, but I understand when you say it's the verbal abuse that hurts the most. It wasn't until I was in college that I learned why he didn't love me. Yet, as cruel as he was to me, when I heard he killed himself, my heart felt as if it would split in two. Guilt overwhelmed me, as if it were my fault for not being there to talk him out of it. After all, as cold-hearted as he was, he was still my daddy, and even after he denied that I was his, I couldn't hate him."

"Keely, I'm so sorry. Thank you for sharing your heart with me."

"Well, girlfriend, I haven't shared my whole heart."

"What d'ya mean?"

"Cami, I'm gonna have a baby."

"A baby?" She squealed with delight. "Oh, m'goodness, Keely, that's awesome."

"Yes it is. The day I was told of Wylie's death, I was also told that I was pregnant. Before I left home that morning, when having my quiet time, I read from Ecclesiastes, third chapter, second verse, where it says—"

Cami smiled. I know the verse well. "There's a time to be born and a time to die."

Keely folded her hands and held them under her chin. "Exactly. That's the one. It was time for Wylie to die and time for a new life to come into the world. It helped me to not only accept Wylie's passing, but to glory in his homegoing."

Cami reached over and grasped her hands. "That's so cool, Keely. I have a favor to ask."

"Anything."

"Would you help me plan my wedding?"

She shrieked. "Wedding? Are you serious? You and Tucker are getting married."

"Yep."

"I'm happy for you both. When's the big day."

"Don't know yet. I'm waiting for him to ask me."

Keely nodded. "Well, we'd better hurry, because I have a feeling it won't be long before he pops the question. He's smitten for sure. This will be so much fun."

"I just hope he'll propose before December. I've always dreamed of a Christmas wedding."

"You don't believe in long engagements, do you? Not that I blame you. Sounds perfect. My baby should be about eight weeks old by then. I'll get to show her . . . or him . . . off at the wedding. Oh, Cami, I've always wanted a sister. I feel as if I've found one."

Cami crooked her pinky. "Soul sisters for life."

CHAPTER 38

Tucker met Cami for lunch at the Hot Dog Shack. He missed his booth at the diner. Change always threw him for a loop. "Are they back yet? You said Friday, and this is Friday. Why aren't they back?"

"They *are* Tucker, and I'm glad, because you've been driving me batty, asking every twenty-four hours, when you knew they weren't due back until today. Mom called last night and said they're home and Bubba plans to open the diner today."

"That's awesome. It's about time. Why did they have to stay a whole week? I'm glad they're back. Meet me at my booth at six o'clock."

She smiled. "*Our* booth."

"Yeah, that's what I meant. But you'll be there?"

"I'll be heading there as soon as I get off work. I can't wait to hear all about their cruise."

****

At five minutes before six, Cami slid into the booth at the diner, and Tucker was there waiting. "I was getting nervous. I thought you weren't coming."

"I told you I'd be here."

"I thought you changed your mind."

"It's barely six, Tucker. It's not as if I'm late." Peculiar, she hadn't thought about it until now, but she hadn't had the weird dreams about Ian—if indeed they were dreams—since meeting Tucker, although she wasn't sure if one had anything to do with the other.

Cami spotted her Mom. "Excuse me, Tuck." She jumped up and ran toward her with open arms. "Welcome back. I don't have to ask if you had fun. It's written all over your face. I can't wait to hear about all the exotic places."

"Oh, honey, we had a fabulous time. I felt eighteen again. It was as if all the past had melted away and we were young again. It was heavenly."

Tucker said, "I need Bubba to come out of the kitchen."

Cami said, "I'm sure he's busy, Tuck."

"This won't take long. Please? It's very important."

"You aren't gonna lecture him on the different styles of cursive, are you?"

"No, I promise. Besides, I've seen his handwriting, and there's nothing to compare it with."

Jackie said, "I'll ask him to step out."

Bubba came out of the kitchen with Jackie, wiping his hands on a dishtowel. Cami stood and gave him a hug. "Thank you."

"For what?"

"For making Mom happy. I've never seen her like this."

Tucker slid out of the booth and reached out for a handshake. "Bubba, how long does it take to get a marriage license and a blood test?"

Bubba glanced at Jackie, who in turn, looked at Cami.

Bubba shrugged. "About three days?"

"Really? That's all? It takes longer than that to get a Driver's License. I waited two weeks before mine came, when I moved from Mississippi."

Cami said, "Tuck, I'm sure that's not what you intended to ask. Bubba's busy. Do you remember why you needed to talk to him?"

"I remember. It's all I thought about all night." Tucker fell to his knees. He wiped perspiration from his upper lip. "Cami Benrey, will you marry me?"

She giggled. "Silly goon, get up. I know you're joking."

Bubba glanced at his wife, then at Cami. "I think he's serious."

Cami's jaw dropped when Tucker pulled a small box from his pocket and flipped it open. She could find no words as she gawked at the huge, pear-shaped diamond, inside the mother-of-pearl box. Her gaze locked with Tucker's.

Bubba threw his head back and hee-hawed. "Well, this is two things I thought I'd never see. Tucker McDowell on his knees in front of a girl, or Cami Benrey, speechless." He said, "Cami, I think the man deserves an answer."

Jackie shot her husband a sideways glance. "This isn't something to enter into lightly, Bubba." She edged closer to her daughter and cupped her hand over her mouth. "Sweetheart, I know you care for him, but you and Tucker have been dating for such a short while. And Asperger's? I know he can't help it, and I have no doubt he's a wonderful young man, but this is a very important step."

"I love him, Mom."

"Sweetheart, it may sound as if I don't like Tucker. I do. But I love you, and as your mother, I'm concerned. Don't act in haste. That's all I'm saying."

Tucker said, "Hel . . .lo. There's someone on the floor waiting for an answer. My knees are getting sore, while you people quibble."

Cami laughed. "Sorry, babe! Yes, yes and yes, I'll marry you, Tucker McDowell. I would be honored to call you my husband." She held out her hand for her fiancé to slip the ring on her finger.

Jackie flashed a cold smile. "Tucker, you do understand if you ever do anything to bring unhappiness to my daughter, I will hunt you down and hurt you bad! Got it?"

Bubba said, "Ooh, Tuck, I wouldn't want to be in your shoes if you crossed this woman."

Tucker stood and when Cami rose, he pulled her close. "Why wouldn't she be happy? Carlos said I was a good catch for any woman. She's lucky to get me."

Jackie's jaw dropped.

Cami draped her arms around his neck and kissed him. "He's messing with you, Mom." Her face twisted when she pushed against his chest with her hand. "You are funning, aren't you, Tuck? Tell her you're kidding."

"Yeah. Just joking. Carlos said 'I shouldn't ever say anything nice about myself. Wait for someone else to do it."

"That's a good rule to remember, babe. My boss is a very smart man."

With his palms out, he looked at Jackie. "Well?"

Jackie clamped her mouth shut, thought, then mumbled, "You have very nice hair, Tucker." She glared at her daughter, and although her lips didn't move, her eyes screamed, "Are you sure you know what you're doing, Camille?"

Cami winked at her Mom, signaling assurance.

Tucker said, "Bubba how much does a marriage license cost?"

Bubba slapped him on the back. "Friend, a marriage license will be the best, but also the cheapest thing you'll be paying for, from hence forward."

Jackie's eyes moistened. "Okay, you two have me convinced. I think I know love when I see it. We have a wedding to plan. June is the perfect month for a wedding. What do you think, sweetie?"

Cami pursed her lips. "I'm thinking December."

"Oh, honey, I know you've wanted a Christmas wedding since you were a little girl, but you might want to reconsider. It's so cold in December. Besides, it's already the first week of October, and we couldn't possibly put a wedding together in two months."

"Mom, I know you mean well, but I plan to have a Christmas wedding."

Jackie grinned. "I learned long ago that if you set your mind, there's no changing it. Okay, so we'll have to begin right away. We'll need to reserve the church, hire a photographer, a wedding planner, and . . ."

"Whoa! Slow down, Mom! Everything is taken care of."

"What do you mean?"

"Keely and I have everything planned, right down to the menu."

"How could you possibly have everything planned, when he just now proposed?"

Cami said, "I had no doubt Tucker would get around to asking, and I knew what my answer would be. I have December 16th, circled on my calendar. We're getting married in Mr. Grimley's big red barn and we'll get Bubba to cater a low-country boil. It'll be so much fun."

Jackie's mouth turned down. "A low-country boil in a barn? Honey, it's your wedding, and I don't mean to throw cold water on your idea, but I'm afraid you haven't put enough thought into this. A barn wedding may sound cute at the moment, but in years to come, you'll regret not having a beautiful church wedding. June is only eight months away, and even that would be rushing things."

"I know you want things perfect for me, Mom, but perfect for me will be a Christmas wedding in a barn." She looked at Tucker and winked. "What do you think about the idea, babe?"

"I wouldn't care if we got married in an outhouse, and the sooner the better. Besides, Christmas is on Sunday this year, and my calendar is already cleared for vacation the week after Christmas. What better way to spend my vacation than honeymooning with my bride? If we marry on Friday night before Christmas, it'll give us an extra weekend for our honeymoon."

Cami squealed. "That's awesome. I didn't think you'd be able to get away."

"I've had it on the calendar since last January. When I scheduled, I thought I'd be going on a safari with a group of doctors, but a honeymoon sounds like a lot more fun."

Cami said, "Okay, so the date is set. Friday night before Christmas. That'll be—" She paused.

Tucker said, "December twenty-third."

"Yes. The twenty-third." Her heart beat like a jackhammer when she repeated the date.

****

Cami attended therapy classes with Tucker, aimed to help him handle compulsive behavior, learn appropriate responses and how to read body language. He was doing much better.

But her—not so good. The wrenching stomach aches and horrific headaches began the moment she agreed to marry Tucker

270

on December 23rd.

Cami lay in bed, with her hand in front of her face. The full moon gave just enough light through the bedroom window for her to admire the gorgeous diamond engagement ring, Tucker had given her. She'd had two very special rings in her lifetime.

She recalled the day Ian put a quarter in a machine and pulled out a cheap little ring, but the joy she felt in her heart when he slid it on her finger was indescribable. Both rings were very special to her, just as the two men in her life were very special.

She tossed and turned, then just as she began to doze off, the bedroom door creaked. Hearing footsteps, she rubbed her eyes and blinked. "Ian?"

He whispered, "Hi babe." He bent down and kissed her.

She pulled the covers back, expecting him to crawl in beside her, the way he'd done on previous visits. Instead, he knelt beside the bed and reached for her hand. Guilt overwhelmed her and the tears flowed. She wanted to tell him everything. Explain that her love for Tucker had not diminished her love for him. Not one iota. He was her first love. She'd always love him. When they repeated their vows at the Court House three years ago, she promised to love him 'til death do us part.' She wanted to tell him she didn't know then, what she'd learned since. Love doesn't stop at death. Love is eternal. They'd only had six short months of life as husband and wife, but she couldn't have loved him more if they'd lived together for a century.

These were the words hidden in her heart, yet when she

attempted to speak, Ian turned and slipped out of the room.

It was so real. Or was it? She rubbed her face. It felt slightly chaffed.

"Ian?" She jumped out of bed and yanked opened the door. But he was gone.

Lexie rolled over in her bed. "Cami? You having a hard time sleeping? It must've been the pizza we had for supper. I've been tossing and turning all night."

Cami sat down on the edge of her roommate's bed. "Are you saying you weren't asleep?"

"I dozed off for a few minutes, but then the noise woke me up."

Her knees knocked. "What noise?"

"I don't suppose it was anything. Goodnight. I'm finally feeling drowsy."

"This is important, Lex. Describe the noise. Did you see anyone?"

Lexie blinked and rubbed her eyes. "See anyone? Of course not. I didn't mean to frighten you. Everything's good, Cami. Go to sleep. It was probably the refrigerator dropping ice into the tray."

She stood and lumbered over to her own bed. "Yeah. I'm sure that's all it was."

But she wasn't sure. She wasn't sure at all.

Camille longed for Ian to come back. Plagued by confusion and guilt, she sobbed. Was she being disloyal to her first love by planning to marry on the date of his death? Should she change her wedding date? Would Tucker understand or would he feel she was putting her feelings for Ian ahead of his feelings. Why did Ian leave so abruptly, without talking to her? If only he'd come back and let her know she had his blessings.

At six o'clock the next morning, Cami called her friend Rydetha in Tennessee and poured out her heart. "What do you think Deedee?"

"Cami, I think it's time you stop torturing yourself. Ian is dead. Dead people don't pay visits in the middle of the night. Surely, you know that, but honey if you continue to have these dreams—hallucinations—whatever they are, then I think it's time for you to seek professional help."

Cami hung up the phone. It wasn't what she wanted to hear, yet, she wasn't sure what she expected Deedee to tell her. *Oh, Ian, I do love Tucker, but I miss you so much.*

CHAPTER 39

December Twenty-third.

As Cami rode in the horse drawn carriage, from the Gentry's Victorian home toward the barn her eyes were drawn to the thousands of twinkling white lights wrapped around the trunks of tall pines, along the path. She could hear the band playing Silent Night, in the distance—her favorite Christmas Carol.

She shivered and pulled the plaid woolen blanket around her shoulders. Her teeth chattered. Though it was a beautiful night, it seemed unusually cold for an Alabama Christmas.

The carriage driver tilted his head upward. "You couldn't have picked a prettier night for a wedding, Miss. Sixty-five degrees and clear skies."

"Sixty-five? Seems much colder."

With a hint of mischief in his eyes, he winked. "Wedding jitters giving you cold feet?"

"Of course not. I suppose it's the wind blowing through the trees, causing it to feel much colder."

The slow, galloping of the horse's hoofs seemed to keep time with the music, which was now becoming slightly louder as they rounded a bend. She hadn't wanted to admit it—not to the driver. Not even to herself. But why? Why now, when there was no going back, was she having these second thoughts? In less than five minutes, she'd be reciting the same vows she recited with Ian. *Till death do us part.* Could she honestly go through it a second time? What was she thinking when she agreed to marry again? And why on December 23rd, of all dates?

When Tucker said his calendar was clear the week after Christmas, and by marrying on Friday, December 23rd, they'd have a full week to enjoy their honeymoon, she agreed, without voicing reservations. After all, it was the only free week he'd have for months, and there was nothing disloyal about marrying her second love on the anniversary death of her first love. At least that's what Rydetha said when Cami asked her opinion. *'Cami, I think it's very apropos that you've chosen to take the saddest day of your life and turn it into the happiest. Doesn't the Bible tell us to put away the bad thoughts and think on that which is good?'* It sounded logical at the time. Not so much, now.

She couldn't deny her lifelong dream had been to have a Christmas wedding. Had she used Tucker's calendar as a convenient excuse to fulfil her dream, in spite of the gnawing gut feeling she was somehow being disloyal to Ian's memory? *This is so wrong. Oh, Ian, please forgive me.* She was about to yell, "Turn around, I can't do this," when the carriage driver said, "You look mighty pretty, ma'am. Dr. McDowell is a very lucky man. Yes'm, he's sure a lucky man."

She swallowed hard. "Thank you." The music grew louder. *Joy to the World the Lord has Come*, rang out, reminding her of Rydetha's words, when she said, "I think it's sweet that you've chosen to turn your mourning into joy."

The carriage stopped and the driver stepped out. He was about to lift her off, when Bubba stepped up, looking like a real cowboy. "Thanks, Frank. I'll get her."

When Bubba put her down, he pecked her on the cheek. "Nervous?"

"Scared to death."

"Thinking of backing out?"

Her lip trembled.

Bubba leaned in. "Cami? Are you okay? You didn't answer me."

"Back out? Never. I love him, so much, Bubba."

"You scared me for a minute. Well, it's time to get this show on the road."

For her wedding dress, Cami had chosen a simple white, long-sleeve sheath and carried a long stem rose, but the biggest expenditure of her wedding attire went on the gorgeous red leather boots.

The barn was filled to capacity, with fifty or more people standing outside. Keely had done an amazing job with the Christmas decorations. It was even lovelier than Cami imagined when they planned it.

Dressed in a pale blue denim skirt and a red-plaid western shirt, Lexie waltzed down the aisle first. Following close behind was Keely, dressed in identical attire, except for one tiny detail. A red sling pouch on her back held a sleeping baby girl.

Trey, the best man, winked as Cami approached the door of the barn, and all the people stood. Bubba crooked his arm. "Are you ready for this?"

She nodded, unable to speak. She glanced from side to side at the crowd, amazed that a barn could hold so many people. Sitting on the pew closest to the entrance, were the Maitre's. Cami's heart was touched, knowing the effort they made to come. What a precious couple. The perfect example of the way God intended marriage to be.

As she and Bubba strolled slowly to the back of the barn, she heard a male's low voice whisper. "Hello, Li'l Darling."

Her throat tightened, seeing Cross-Tee sitting with a row of bikers in durags.

Her heart raced when she looked up and stared into the eyes of her handsome husband-to-be. Such a brilliant man with a heart of gold. Was he perfect? Almost. Tucker didn't have a mean bone in his body, yet his penchant for honesty—a consequence of the Asperger's—sometimes landed him in trouble. How ironic that most people have to learn to be truthful, while Tuck spent hours in therapy, learning when not to be. Asperger's had its problems, but neither lying nor manipulation was among them. She would always be able to count on her darling husband being open and honest about everything. How many women could tout that about their husbands? What a precious man. How could one girl be so blessed as to find two such wonderful men in one short lifetime?

Johnny Gorham stepped up to the microphone, prepared to sing the same song he sang at Bubba and Jackie's wedding. Cami had grown up hearing her mother sing *Only You*, an old song by a group that called themselves The Platters. Before Johnny sang it at the Knox wedding, he had announced it was Jackie and Bubba's love song, back when they were very young and so much in love.

Johnny sang it so beautifully at her mom's wedding, Cami had requested him to sing it for her and Tucker. What was she thinking? A lump the size of a golf ball stuck in her throat when Johnny's mellow voice crooned, "*You are my destiny, my one and only you.*" As many times as she'd heard the song, today it took on a completely different meaning. If she understood the meaning of destiny, it described one's life as being predetermined by a set of inevitable events.

How could that be? If Tucker was indeed her destiny,

predetermined to be her one and only, did it mean Ian's death was unavoidable because he made the fatal mistake of falling in love with someone destined to be with another? It seemed so unfair if Ian had to die for her and Tucker's life purpose to be fulfilled. She rubbed her temples. Where were these confusing thoughts coming from?

When the preacher asked, "Who gives this woman," Bubba glanced at his wife and winked. He proudly proclaimed, "Her mother and I." Cami gazed into Tucker's glistening brown eyes—eyes that confirmed she was his everything—his one and only. All the doubts and confusion melted away. Her warm heart cried out, *"It is only you, Tucker . . . but once, a lifetime ago, it was only Ian. Oh, Ian. If I could only be assured, had you known, you would've given your blessings.*

A verse in Psalms, she learned as a child—yet couldn't recall ever having an occasion to use it—popped in her mind, ushering in a comforting sense of peace. *"The Lord will perfect that which concerneth me."* God said it in his word and His word was truth. Perfection would work just fine. It didn't say he *has* perfected, but rather, He *will* perfect.

The brief ceremony went off without a hitch. After the wedding, Cami thanked Cross-Tee and his friends for taking the time to attend her wedding. She hadn't ceased to be amazed at how their chance meeting had come about at Deal's Gap. What were the odds? She trembled to think how differently the trip to Mobile could've turned out, had it not been for these awesome guys who served as her protectors. But was it really by chance or could it have been a divine appointment? It wasn't the first time she'd put her life in jeopardy. Her thoughts traveled back to the day she stood alongside an Interstate, when a handsome biker pulled up and refused to leave her there alone.

As they rode away, Cami blinked. Then blinked again. Though there was a monstrous cloud of dust obscuring a clear view, the trailing bike looked exactly like Ian's. Naturally, he wasn't the only biker with a blue Harley Road King. However, it was the biker's helmet that made her breath catch in her throat. *A half-heart? Impossible.* She squinted her eyes, but the thick cloud of dust hindered her vision as they rode out of sight.

A vivid memory of another sudden cloud of dust flooded her thoughts—the first day she met Ian, when he slammed to a stop between her and the pavement, causing dust to fill her eyes, her nostrils and her mouth.

Tucker reached down on the ground and picked up a tiny metal object. "Would you look at this? The guy riding point dropped this little trinket, when he waved goodbye. I saw it as it sailed from his hands."

"What is it?"

"A tiny bell with a cross." He twisted it around in his hands. "Interesting. I'm sure there's sentimental value attached to this little gadget, because it has the International Baccalaureate logo inscribed on the inside." He handed it to his bride.

Her voice quivered with emotion. "It's a Guardian Bell."

"A what?"

"A Guardian Bell."

"So, you've seen others like this?"

"I've seen one exactly like this. There's a legend that whoever receives a Guardian Bell as a gift will receive a double portion of blessings."

"I've heard of Guardian Angels, but never Guardian Bells." Tucker placed his arm around her shoulder. "I believe in Guardian Angels. I think we all have one. What about you, Cami? Do you believe?"

Her vision blurred from moisture filling her eyes. "Most definitely. I believe it with all my heart." She gazed at the initials. *IB? International Baccalaureate? . . . or Ian Benrey?"*

"Hey, you're crying."

"They're happy tears, Tucker. You are an amazing man and I'm so grateful God brought you into my life. I love you more than you'll ever know."

"I hope I can always make you happy, Cami. When we get back from our honeymoon, we'll buy you a nice silver chain and you can wear the bell around your neck. If your friend rides back through, you can let him know he dropped it."

"The chain is a great idea, babe, but I think I'll put it on my bike. We won't ever see him again."

"You never know."

Clutching the tiny bell, she gazed into the clouds and murmured. "Oh, but I do. Besides, he didn't drop it by accident, sweetheart. It was his gift to us."

"Cool. According to the legend, we should be doubly blessed. You don't really believe that, though, do you?"

"I'm sure of it, sweetheart. It's worked for me already."

Made in the USA
Columbia, SC
13 October 2020